The Haunted Bones

A LIN COFFIN

COZY MYSTERY

BOOK 3

J.A. WHITING

COPYRIGHT 2016 J.A. WHITING

Cover copyright 2016 Signifer Book Design

Formatting by Signifer Book Design

Proofreading by Donna Rich

This book is a work of fiction. Names, characters, places, or incidents are products of the author's imagination or are used fictitiously. Any resemblance to locales, actual events, or persons, living or dead, is entirely coincidental.

All rights reserved.

No part of this publication can be reproduced or transmitted in any form or by any means, electronic or mechanical, without permission in writing from J. A. Whiting.

To hear about new books and book sales, please sign up for my mailing list at: www.jawhitingbooks.com

For the loved ones who watch over us

CHAPTER 1

Carolin Coffin leaned back against her front door and yawned. Her little mixed breed dog sat beside her on the front landing of the house pressing his body against her arm. She grinned at him. "You can lie down on the step, you know. I'd do the same thing, but people driving by might think something was wrong with me if I fell asleep in front of my own house."

Although Lin and the dog had been up since 6am, she was pretty sure he'd slept at least half of the day while she had been out with her boyfriend, Jeff. Her leg muscles felt sore from their thirty-mile bike ride around the island of Nantucket. They'd stopped for lunch at Surfside beach and spent two hours bobbing in the ocean swells and body-surfing in the waves. When they returned to Lin's house, they took the friendly dog on a two-hour walk on some trails in a wooded section of the island.

Lin absent-mindedly fiddled with the gold pendant around her neck as she pictured her handsome boyfriend. The necklace was once owned by her ancestor, Emily Witchard Coffin and it was found in her cousin Viv's storage shed hidden there hundreds of years ago by Emily's husband, Sebastian, an early settler of Nantucket.

In the center of the pendant was a white-gold horseshoe which tilted slightly to one side. The design of the horseshoe could be seen in the chimney bricks of several old houses on the island and was intended to ward off witches and evil spells. Sebastian and Emily Coffin used the symbol on their own chimney to draw people who had been accused of witchcraft to their home in order to give them a safe place to stay as they settled on the island.

Viv gave Emily Coffin's horseshoe necklace to Lin because she and Emily shared the same skill, Lin and her ancestor could both see ghosts.

The dog yawned and Lin chuckled. "I guess those little legs of yours have to work a lot harder than mine when we go on walks."

The heat of the August day was starting to fade and a refreshing breeze coming off the sea cooled Lin's skin. She shifted on the cement step and her lower back gave a twinge. "I'm going to be sore tomorrow." Lin shook her head thinking about the heavy work that was planned for the next day with Leonard, her landscaping partner.

She heard his truck approaching and she turned her head and waved. When the man pulled up to the curb, the dog's little stump of a tail jiggled back and forth and he let out a soft woof of welcome.

Lin opened the passenger side door of the truck and Nicky leaped inside.

"You bringin' that cur with you again?" Leonard tried to be gruff, but he couldn't stifle a grin as the small, lovable creature wiggled and attempted to lick the man's face. "Okay, okay." He reached down and scratched the dog's ears. Leonard was tall, slim, and fit and although he had plenty of gray mixed in with his brown hair, Lin couldn't believe it when she found out that he was in his early sixties.

"You look beat, Coffin." Leonard started the truck and pulled away from the house.

"That's because I am." Lin smiled as they sped along. She looked out the window at the pretty gray-shingled cottages lining the road, the people riding bikes on the bike paths that wound around the island, and families, friends, and couples strolling along the sidewalks heading into town. A contented sigh slipped from her throat.

Lin and Leonard had recently joined forces and started a new landscaping business together. Although the two got along well and had become friends, things hadn't started out that way. When Lin first met the man, he was in a bad way, and she suspected him as the killer in a murder that had occurred early in the summer.

Leonard had been stabbed by the real perpetrator when he went to Lin's house to warn her. Guilty and ashamed for dismissing him as a creep, Lin visited him in the hospital and got to know him. Leonard had lost his wife many years ago in a tragic accident and every summer around the anniversary of her death, he fell into depression, drinking, not eating right, and letting personal hygiene fall by the wayside. Each year, with a mighty struggle, he'd managed to pull himself out of the funk.

From the corner of her eye, Lin peeked at Leonard, clean-shaven and neatly dressed in a collared shirt and chinos, and she smiled. He'd made it out of his grief for another year.

Nicky sat on Lin's lap with his nose reaching up to the two-inch opening in the window. She turned to her business partner. "So what's this place like?"

Leonard turned the truck onto the road that would take them to the mid-island property that they'd been contracted to landscape. "It's a pretty place, old. The new owners wanted a family room off the back of the house. The construction just finished last week so now they want the yard cleaned up and taken care of. It's the usual post-construction mess. Mounds of soil, grass ripped up. We'll need one of those small front loaders to move the dirt around. I ordered one. It was supposed to be dropped off this afternoon."

Lin's eyes twinkled. "Ohhh. A mini front loader?" She rubbed her hands together. "I've always wanted to operate one of those."

"Well, you're about to get your wish." Leonard turned the truck onto a dirt lane and the vehicle bumped over the uneven surface jostling its occupants. Rounding a bend in the long driveway and emerging from the grove of woods, the sprawling farmhouse-style home came into view.

"Wow, it's beautiful." Lin leaned forward in the passenger seat and stared through the windshield. "When was it built?"

"Eighteen hundreds. It's been well-taken care of." Leonard eased the truck to a stop in front of a garage to the right of the house. The garage had been built in the style of an old barn.

Lin, Leonard, and Nicky stepped out of the truck and headed for the front door.

"I love this place." Lin looked all around. "It's such a great house."

The two climbed the steps to the front porch and rang the bell. No one answered. "I told the owners we'd be coming by. They said they probably wouldn't be here. They're not around much." Leonard left the porch. "Let's go out back."

The rear of the house was exactly as Leonard had described it. A mess.

"Ugh." Lin groaned as she stood behind the new family room addition and turned in a small circle looking over the yard. "We've got our work cut out for us." Mounds of soil stood like a small mountain range on one side of the yard. The main section of the space looked like a tractor, or two, had scraped up every blade of grass and dumped dirt and mud in its place. "I think we better bring in some help."

"I'm on it. I talked to Dave and Remy about working with us. They're onboard."

"Thank heavens." Lin exhaled in relief. Dave and Remy were a husband-wife team in their forties who had been contracting with Lin and Leonard to help out on new projects. The couple were easy to get along with and weren't afraid of hard work.

Lin had seen the plans for the yard and she and Leonard walked around discussing what had to be done and what should be tackled first as Nicky ran from side to side, his nose to the ground sniffing at all the new scents.

A rumbling sound could be heard in front of the house. "Must be the front loader."

"Tomorrow's my lucky day." Lin grinned at Leonard. "You might not get to drive it at all, you know."

Leonard walked around to the front of the house to meet the delivery driver while Lin remained in the yard. She took a notebook out of her bag and wrote down some notes about which landscaping tasks should be completed first and what they'd need to bring to work tomorrow. Nicky continued his running and sniffing.

Lin moved towards the side property line and startled.

Between the branches and foliage she could make out a man standing in his yard staring over at

Lin. She was about to lift her hand in a greeting when the person did an abrupt about-face and walked away. Lin frowned and gave a slight shrug wondering about the man's unfriendly manner. She thought maybe he was embarrassed to have been caught watching her and pretended not to see her.

The sun was low in the sky and the yard was darkening. A chilly breeze touched Lin's skin and made her shiver. "Nick?" The dog had run behind one of the dirt mounds. Lin glanced towards the front of the house wondering what was taking Leonard so long. Feeling uneasy and not understanding why, she forced herself to complete her inspection of the yard.

Acres of woods enclosed the garden area at the back of the property. Lin usually liked the feeling of quiet and privacy when a yard was ringed by trees. The woods provided a nice backdrop to a space that was landscaped with natural plants and flowers which was what the new owners of the farmhouse had requested. Lin had looked forward to working on the project, but something was pricking at her. She let out a long breath, annoyed with her feelings of uneasiness, and moved her gaze along the periphery of the yard, not really knowing what she expected to see. Shrugging a shoulder, she turned abruptly and walked back towards the house.

Lin noticed she hadn't seen the dog for a while. "Nick?"

She heard a whine from behind one of the dirt piles and headed in that direction. "What are you doing, Nicky?" A sudden rush of coldness flooded her core and she stopped in her tracks.

The dog whined again from behind the mounds of soil.

Lin flicked her eyes to the side of the house hoping to see Leonard returning, but he was still out front. She called to her dog and when he didn't appear, a flash of unease ran down her back. *What's wrong with me?* She straightened and moved to the other side of the dirt hills.

Lin let out a sigh of relief when she spotted the dog busily digging in the dirt. "Come on, Nick. It's time to go."

The dog lifted his head, holding something in his mouth.

"What have you got there?" She stepped closer. "Did you find a bone?" She chuckled. "Well, some dog is not going to be happy with you for stealing his bone."

Nicky dropped the object and whined. He stared at Lin.

A whoosh of cold air engulfed her. She inched closer to the dog and bent down, reaching for the thing that the little animal had found. Lin lifted the good-sized, whitish-gray bone and turned it over in her hands. At first, her fingers felt like they were touching ice, and then it seemed like tiny sparks were biting into her hand. Her heart sank.

Oh, no.

Lin flicked her eyes to the edge of the yard.

The ghost of Emily Witchard Coffin stood staring at her ... and the bone.

CHAPTER 2

Lin stood up holding the bone in her hand. The shimmering ghost held Lin's eyes and then shifted her gaze to the bone in the young woman's hand. Lin glanced down at the object in her grip and a wave of icy air caused her to shudder.

Leonard came around the pile of dirt and saw Lin and the dog. "What are you doin' there, Coffin? Diggin' for bones?" He chuckled and walked over. Leaning down, he patted the dog's head. "Hey, Nick. Did you find some other dog's bone?"

"I don't think it's a dog's buried treasure. I think it's too big." Lin held it out for Leonard to inspect.

"What do you mean?" The man looked warily at the thing in Lin's hand.

Lin took a quick glance at Emily who was still standing by the property line and then she looked around to see if Emily's husband, Sebastian, had made an appearance. She didn't see him anywhere in the yard.

Lin's face clouded and her lips turned down. "I think it's human. I think it's a human bone."

Leonard let out a snort of disbelief. "It can't be human, maybe deer or bear or something like that."

Lin tilted her head, a disbelieving look on her face.

"A previous owner could have been a hunter, dumped the bones in the yard." Leonard waved his hand around at the space. "The construction of the addition brought stuff up to the surface. It happens all the time."

"Bones? All the time?"

"Not *all* the time." Leonard ran his hand over his hair. "Sometimes." He looked at Lin. "It can't be human."

Lin wished he was right. Taking a quick glance at Emily and seeing the expression on the ghost's face, Lin knew it wasn't an animal bone. She let out a sigh. "We need to call the police. Let them know we found a bone in the yard."

Leonard groaned and pulled his phone out. After reporting the find to the police, he listened for a few moments and then clicked off. "They're coming now. We have to wait."

"Let's go wait on the front porch." Lin was still holding the bone. "What should I do with it?"

"Bring it out front." Leonard didn't seem to want to touch it.

"Good idea. It's getting dark." Lin looked around the yard. "We don't want an animal to come by and make off with it."

"Come on. I'll show you the piece of equipment

that got delivered."

The two headed for the front of the house with the dog trailing behind. Lin's excitement about driving the mini front loader had faded, having been replaced with an unfocused sense of worry and unease. The more she tried to brush the concern from her mind, the more it stood front and center.

In less than twenty minutes, a police car came around the corner while Leonard was showing Lin how the front loader worked. When the officers stepped out of the car, Lin explained how and where she'd found the bone. In the gathering darkness, she gestured to the porch where she'd left the object and the officers went to inspect it.

The police officers flicked on flashlights and after taking a close look, they straightened. "We'll deliver it to the medical examiner's office to get a determination on whether or not it's human."

Lin walked to the back of the farmhouse to point out where the dog had been digging. She looked over her shoulder to see if Emily or Sebastian Coffin were lingering in the yard. To her relief, there were no ghostly apparitions watching them. After a few minutes, the police finished the brief inspection. "We'll get some forensics people out here tomorrow if the bone turns out to be human. We'll speak to the owners of the property and let them know what's going on."

One officer said, "You can't do any landscaping

work back here until the okay is given."

"How long will that take?" Lin looked worried. She and Leonard were on a tight schedule to finish this project and move to the next one. A lengthy delay would throw a monkey wrench into their plans.

The officer shrugged. "Depends."

***

Leonard dropped Lin and Nicky off at her house. They decided that tomorrow they'd each work on some of the small projects on their list of clients. That way they could clear some time at the end of the week to focus solely on the farmhouse landscaping job, hopeful that by then the police would have finished their investigation.

"You don't think they'll find any other bones, do you?" Lin asked Leonard as they headed home in the truck.

"Nah. Well, maybe, if like I said, a hunter once lived at the house and used the yard to dump the bones. They'll figure out pretty quick that the thing is an animal bone. Then we can get back to work."

Once inside her house, Lin showered and changed clothes and texted her cousin to see if she'd like to come over for a late dinner. While waiting for Viv, Lin worked in her small office which was the home's second bedroom doing computer programming work. Before moving back to Nantucket, she arranged to work remotely on a part-time basis for her previous employer.

Viv arrived at Lin's house with her huge gray and white cat, Queenie. The cat and dog touched noses and ran to the doggy-door to head outside to the field behind Lin's cottage. The girls made a salad and put some leftover lasagna into the oven to warm.

Viv poured a glass of wine for herself and opened a bottle of craft beer for her cousin. They perched on stools in front of the kitchen island sipping their drinks. Lin told Viv about the unusual discovery in the rear yard of her new client's home.

"A bone?" Viv scrunched up her nose. "You mean like a chicken bone or something?"

"No. Like a big bone." Lin lifted her beer glass to her lips.

"How big was it?"

When Lin described the length and heft of the bone, Viv looked horrified. "What could that be? A deer leg?" Her blue eyes flashed.

Lin didn't say anything for a few moments, and then she looked her cousin in the eye. "I saw Emily Coffin there. Right after Nicky found the bone."

The wine glass almost slipped from Viv's fingers and a few drops of liquid plopped onto the countertop. "Emily? Oh, no." She wiped her spill with a dishtowel.

On their mothers' side, the two girls were descended from the same branch of the Witchard family, early settlers of Nantucket, but paternally, Lin was a descendant of Sebastian Coffin while Viv came from a different branch of the Coffin family.

Viv knew that her cousin could see ghosts and readily accepted it, but sometimes it frightened her when spirits showed themselves to Lin. With the help of the ghosts, Viv and Lin had recently solved two mysteries on the island. Viv told her cousin that two mysteries in a lifetime were plenty for her and she hoped never to be involved in another case.

"Why was Emily Coffin there?" Worry lines creased the corners of Viv's eyes.

Lin sighed. "Leonard is sure the bone belongs to an animal. But when I saw Emily there, I pretty much knew it was a human bone." She gave a slight shrug. "Why else would Emily appear?"

"Oh, no." Viv's voice trembled.

Lin couldn't help the corners of her mouth turning up. "Nothing's happened yet," she offered, trying to calm her worried cousin. "Maybe Emily just came by to say hello."

Viv leveled her eyes at Lin. "Right." She picked up her wine glass and shimmied it a little to swirl the red liquid around. "If it *is* a bone from a person ... why is it there? I suppose it could be old. Maybe there was a person a long time ago who was buried in the backyard after he or she passed away. Maybe there isn't anything horrible about it. No murder, nothing like that."

"Maybe."

"But you don't think so?"

Lin raised an eyebrow. "I don't think people were buried in their backyards. Even years ago, there were burial grounds on the island. If someone was buried behind their house, then I'd think foul play was involved. And, honestly? I think that we might have bumped up against something today that's going to turn out to be trouble."

"Oh, no," Viv said for the third time in five minutes.

"We'll just have to wait and see." Lin got up and removed the lasagna pan from the oven. The girls scooped out portions and placed them on plates. They added salad and dressing and carried everything out to sit at the table on the deck. Lin lit some candles that stood in glass containers in the center of the table.

"I was glad you hadn't had dinner when I texted." Lin sprinkled some ground Parmesan and Romano cheese on the top of her meal. "It was so late. I thought you would have eaten already."

"The bookstore was really busy today, so I stayed later than I planned to." Viv owned a bookstore-café in the center of Nantucket town. "When I was walking home, John called and asked if I could meet him at a house showing." Viv's boyfriend was an island Realtor and last month when he was showing a house to a couple, he opened the door to the first floor bathroom to discover a dead body.

Ever since the gruesome discovery, John had been having problems showing unoccupied real estate and he would ask Viv or a friend or his brother to accompany him to a showing that he couldn't get out of. Lin even went with him once when everyone else was occupied.

"Is his anxiety getting any better?" Lin swallowed a bite of her meal.

"No." Viv shook her head. "He's fine with houses that are occupied. The empty homes are the ones that cause the issue. They remind him too much of the house where he found the body. And he still won't set foot on that street either." Viv scratched the ears of her cat who had returned from the back field with Nicky. "That's why I hadn't eaten yet."

Lin got up from the deck chair and went inside the house. She brought out some cookies that she'd made the day before. Even though they both had to get up early in the morning for work, the girls made tea and sat outside a while longer enjoying the warm August air, the peaceful night, and the tasty cookies.

Neither one said so, but they each had the feeling that "peaceful" wasn't how they'd be describing the days ahead.

CHAPTER 3

Lin and Jeff sat on a blanket eating their lunches in the shade of a huge Maple tree at the wooded edge of a small island cemetery. Jeff, a carpenter and handyman, was working in the area where Lin had just finished up mowing and trimming a client's lawn when they texted each other and decided to meet up for lunch. Lin handed Nicky a carrot dipped in hummus and he eagerly chomped it.

"I didn't know dogs liked carrots and hummus." Jeff chuckled as he leaned against the trunk of the tree.

The day was hot and humid and they both appreciated the coolness of the shady spot. Lin handed Jeff a plastic bowl and a bottle of water from her small cooler. He poured the water into the dish and set it down for the dog. As Lin and Jeff munched on their sandwiches, she told him about visiting the new landscaping project last evening with Leonard.

"A bone? Chances are it's an animal." Jeff took a long swig from his water bottle. "I hope it doesn't take them long to determine that it's not human so you can get started on the yard. There's a lot to do on that job."

Lin nodded in agreement. "Even a couple of days of waiting will set us back. We really need to keep on schedule. It's a new business and we want to be sure to make good impressions on our clients."

Lin had not shared any information about her ability to see ghosts with her new boyfriend. Even though she wished he knew, she wasn't yet ready to tell him, so she couldn't reveal that she had seen the ghost of Emily Coffin while at the farmhouse. She would have liked to talk things over with him and express her worry about seeing Emily right after discovering the bone and what it might mean.

"Are you okay?" Jeff asked wondering about Lin's more subdued demeanor.

Lin smiled. "Yeah, just thinking about how to adjust our schedule to keep all of our projects on track." She offered Jeff one of the cookies she'd made and tried to shake off her concern about the bone. Lin rested back on the blanket and looked up at the sky between the branches of the tree. "We should meet for lunch more often."

Jeff leaned down and kissed the pretty brunette. "I agree. It's nice to see you in the middle of the day."

"This is such a peaceful spot." Lin could feel the tension draining out of her muscles. Nicky settled down on the blanket next to her. Lin had contracted with the manager of the small town cemetery to mow and trim and plant and take care of the flowers around the entrance. It was one of the very first clients she acquired when she moved back to Nantucket in June. The mid-island spot was surrounded by mature trees and had shady lanes running in a criss-cross pattern leading to nicely-tended plots. It was one of the oldest cemeteries on the island. Because of its vegetation and position on a bluff, the cemetery was often cooler than other spots in the area. There were often people from the nearby neighborhood taking walks or pushing strollers along the lanes.

"I learned to drive here." Jeff smiled recalling his father giving him directions and sometimes gripping the dashboard when he took too close of a turn. "It was a good place to get the hang of driving, not many other cars around, a chance to practice turning, getting a feel for handling a vehicle without actually being out on a road."

Lin chuckled. "I learned to drive in a cemetery, too."

Jeff looked out over the grounds. "It's probably pretty entertaining for any spirits hanging around to watch the nervous parents teaching their kids, cars jerking and lurching, some close calls running into low-hanging branches and getting too close to the bushes."

Lin shook her head and kidded, "I was never

such an awful driver."

"Is that right?" Jeff looked skeptical. "If he was still alive, I bet your grandfather would have something else to say on the subject."

"He'd agree with me." As Lin sat up and reached for her water, her phone hummed with an incoming call. She murmured a few "I sees" and "okays" before saying "thank you" and ending the call. Shifting on the blanket to face Jeff, she let out a sigh. "It was a police officer from last evening. He said the bone is human."

"Oh." Jeff's eyebrows shot up in surprise. "I didn't expect that."

"Leonard and I can't start work at the farmhouse until an investigation is completed. They have to do a search for more bones."

"That can't take long." Jeff tried to reassure Lin. "You shouldn't have to wait too long before you can start the job."

Lin rolled her eyes. "I hope." Her heart rate had increased while she was on the call and a sense of heaviness fell over her. She had been dreading the news about the bone because she was pretty sure it would turn out to be human. "I wonder how it got there. I wonder what happened."

"Maybe it's old. It might have been there for decades."

"Let's hope so." Lin ran her hand over her forehead. "We don't need any more mysteries."

Nicky stood up and whined. Jeff reached over

and patted the dog's head. "What's the matter, boy?"

A cool breeze fluttered over Lin's skin and she froze for a second. Slowly, she shifted and looked towards the small grassy incline across the road from where they were sitting. Emily Coffin stood staring at them. Lin coughed to mask her sudden intake of air. She took a swallow of water and turned her eyes to the spot where the ghost stood. The two made eye contact and then Emily shimmered in the sunlight and faded away.

"I'd better be getting back to work." Jeff scrunched up his sandwich wrapper and placed it in his lunch box.

Lin stood and gathered her things. She lifted the blanket, shook it, and folded it into thirds. They started down the path through the woods to the road where they'd left their vehicles. The tree branches made a canopy over the trail and the wooded area was cool and shady. Walking along, Lin's mind jumped from one thought to the next. *Whose bone is it? How did it get in the ground behind the farmhouse? How long has it been there? Who put it there? Where are the rest of the person's bones? Am I about to get sucked into this?*

A strange sensation washed over Lin and she stopped short, her head spinning.

Jeff took three more steps and then looked around. "What's wrong? Did you leave something under the tree?"

Lin's ears buzzed. She blinked. "What?"

"Why did you stop?"

"I...." Lin tried to shake off the odd feeling of dizziness. "I don't know. I felt funny for a second."

Jeff put his hand on her arm. "It's probably the heat. Do you want to sit down?"

Lin put her hand over his. "I'm okay." She smiled. "I should drink more water. Maybe I got a tiny bit dehydrated."

The two held hands as they continued down the path. Lin took a quick glance over her shoulder expecting Emily to be standing behind them, but the ghost wasn't there. She felt the pull of something, almost like a sensation of being watched. *It must just be because Emily showed herself back there.*

If Jeff wasn't with her, Lin would have turned around and walked back along the trail. She decided that after finishing up the lawn mowing at the cemetery, she might take another walk along the path.

They reached the end of the short trail where their trucks were parked off the road on a hard-packed sandy strip. Lin opened the passenger side door so the dog could jump in. She tossed the blanket and her lunch cooler in the back and then walked over to Jeff's truck. "Can you come to Viv's for dinner tomorrow night?"

"I wouldn't miss it." The handsome carpenter took the pretty brunette in his arms and they shared a sweet kiss. "Are you okay? Has the dizziness passed?'

Lin nodded. "I'm fine."

"Remember to drink plenty of water while you're working." Jeff pushed a tendril of Lin's hair behind her ear. "Call me if you feel funny."

"I will. I'll be okay."

The two parted ways and Lin climbed into her truck to move it around to the cemetery entrance so she could remove her equipment and begin her work. She placed sound protecting headphones over her ears, stepped onto the lawn mower platform, started it up, and put it into gear. She waved at the manager who was walking towards his office and began to mow the stretch of lawn closest to where she and Jeff had eaten lunch. Zooming past the entrance to the trail they'd walked along to their vehicles, Lin experienced another sudden bout of near dizziness and she gripped tight to the mower's handles. She shook her head and tried to relax her shoulder muscles.

Glancing back at the path through the woods, an overwhelming sense of dread flooded her body and she decided to skip having another look at the trail when she'd finished her work. The feeling made her think that something was wrong at the cemetery, but there was no way she wanted to investigate on her own.

She'd have to convince Viv to come back with her later.

CHAPTER 4

"It's human?" Viv frowned. "Oh, no." The girls sat on Viv's deck sipping some homemade lemonade mixed with iced tea and nibbling on tortilla chips and salsa. Nicky and Queenie lay side by side on the deck keeping watch over the back lawn in case a chipmunk or squirrel got the bold idea that they could meander through the yard. "That's why Emily Coffin showed up behind the farmhouse. She knew it was a human bone."

"There has to be a reason that Emily was standing there. If it was just a bone of someone who died of natural causes and was buried in the farmhouse yard, she wouldn't have appeared." Lin took a gulp of her drink. "So there's something amiss. Unfortunately."

"Emily must want you to look into it."

Lin lifted her eyes to her cousin as she dipped a chip to scoop up some salsa. "I was afraid of that." She bit her chip and chewed slowly. "But what can I do? The police will start an investigation. They're far better equipped to look into it."

"Well, Emily must want you to do something about it." Viv went to check on the burritos in the oven.

Lin looked out over the garden spilling with perennial and annual flowers. Her cousin definitely had a green thumb. The sun had slipped behind the tops of the tallest trees and the day's heat began to lessen its grip. When Viv returned to the deck, Lin complimented her on how nice the garden looked. "Maybe you should give up running the bookstore and join me and Leonard in the landscaping business."

Viv rolled her blue eyes and groaned. "That would require too much physical labor." She shook her head. "Nope, not my cup of tea." Placing a tray with salad and salad plates onto the deck table, she said, "I prefer to be inside in the nice, cool air conditioned space, not rolling around in the dirt in the heat of the day. Besides, I can dress cute at the bookstore and I don't look great in shorts and a tank top."

"I would disagree." Lin smiled. "I bet John would disagree, too."

"Love is blind." Viv headed back into the house and Lin followed to help carry the dinner plates and silverware outside.

When they were settled in their chairs with hearty portions of salad and burritos, they dug in to the delicious Mexican food. After munching in silence for a few minutes, Lin leaned back in her seat. "Jeff and I met for lunch today."

"Oohh. Where did you go? Somewhere nice by the water?"

Lin grinned. "We ate on a blanket under a tree in Mid-Island Cemetery."

"Really?" Viv tilted her head to the side, a look of distaste on her face. "How romantic."

"It was actually very nice and peaceful. It was the spur of the moment. I was scheduled to mow the cemetery lawn so Jeff met me there." A cloud passed over Lin's face.

"Usually when you talk about Jeff you smile." Viv eyed her cousin. "What happened?"

Lin shook herself. "Nothing. We had a nice time."

"But, what?" Viv cut a piece of her burrito and gave some to Nicky and the cat.

"Well...." Lin paused.

"I knew it." Viv crossed her arms on the table and leaned forward. "What happened?"

Lin sucked in a breath. "Jeff and I walked back to our trucks through the woods along a trail that leads to the road. We left the trucks there. We didn't want to park inside the cemetery entrance since it's so small. It's a tight little lane and I didn't want to block it. I have to park inside the gate when I work and I pull the truck way over to the side."

Viv's eyebrow went up. "You don't need to go on and on about where you parked."

"I'm telling you why we happened to be on the trail."

Viv waved her hand to encourage Lin to go on with the story.

"So, when we were walking along the path going back to the trucks, I got a really weird sensation."

Viv's lips pursed and eyes went wide. "What kind of a sensation?" Her voice was cautious.

"I felt dizzy. Like the woods were spinning." Lin put her hand on her temple and rubbed. She looked at Viv, her heart starting to pound. "I felt like someone was watching me."

"Maybe it was Emily?"

Lin shook her head. "It wasn't her. It wasn't the same feeling."

"Did you look around? Maybe someone was walking in the woods."

Lin let out a sigh. "I did glance around. I didn't see anyone."

The girls sat thinking in silence. Nicky let out a loud, sudden whine and the two cousins jumped. Viv chuckled. "We're not nervous at all, are we?" She reached down and gave the dog a pat. "Funny dog."

When Viv straightened up, she saw Lin staring at her. "What?" Viv's cheek twitched. "Oh, no. I know what you're thinking."

"What am I thinking?"

"You want to go back to that cemetery and look around."

A smile crept over Lin's lips. "I guess you know me pretty well."

Viv squared her shoulders. "I'm not going. No."

"Come on. I don't want to go there alone."

"Take Nicky and Queenie. They'll protect you."

Lin didn't say anything.

Viv said, "It's dark. You won't be able to see a thing."

"I have a flashlight." Lin focused her gaze on her cousin.

"Why does everything have to happen at night?" Viv pushed her hair behind her ear. "Why don't we go during the day when other people are around?"

"Because you work in the bookstore all day and I have lawns to mow and flowers to plant," Lin said.

"Oh, okay." Viv lifted her fork with a heavy sigh. "At least let me finish my meal."

"Thank you." Lin smiled. "I really didn't want to go there alone."

Viv placed a dollop of sour cream on top of her burrito. "I know I'll end up regretting this."

"Eating the sour cream?" Lin kidded.

"No." Viv leveled her eyes. "Our moonlight cemetery visit."

Lin chuckled and finished the last swallow of her lemonade-iced tea. "I'll go clean up the kitchen while you finish eating." She called to the cat and dog to follow her inside. "We're all going on an outing," she told them with a big smile.

Viv groaned.

***

By the time the dishes were loaded into the dishwasher, the leftovers were put away, and the foursome climbed into Lin's truck, the sun had set and darkness covered the island. After a twenty-minute drive, Lin pulled the vehicle to the side of the road near the trail she parked next to earlier in the day with Jeff. "Here we are."

Viv stared out of the passenger side window. "It is pitch black out here. We're going to walk in the woods?"

Lin opened her door and slid out. "We were about halfway down the path when I got the odd feeling." She removed a large black flashlight from her toolbox that was kept in the truck bed and clicked it on. The white-yellow light brightened a spot on the path and Lin and Viv started down the trail. Nicky and Queenie had their noses to the ground as they scurried along, sniffing. Some moonlight filtered through the trees' branches and pooled here and there on the ground.

Viv looked over her shoulder and rubbed her arms with her hands. "It's cool."

"It's just your fear," Lin teased her cousin to lighten the atmosphere since she didn't want to admit how nervous and uneasy she was feeling about their evening stroll.

Some twigs scrunched underfoot. An animal could be heard moving in the wooded section next to them.

"You don't think it's a bear, do you?" Viv whispered. She squinted towards the sound.

"Probably just a serial killer." Lin got an elbow in the ribs for that comment.

As they proceeded down the dark path, Lin's skin shivered from the sensation of cold. "I feel cold air."

"Do you see any ghosts?" Viv kept her voice down.

Lin glanced around while shining the flashlight beam between the trees. "Not yet." Continuing further along the trail, Lin suddenly reached her hand out and grabbed her cousin's arm. "I feel it. I feel dizzy again." They halted.

Viv's head spun side to side trying to see the cause of her cousin's distress. "I don't see anything." She held tight to Lin's arm.

"Let's keep walking. See if the feeling gets stronger."

They emerged out of the woods and onto the edge of the cemetery. "I can feel it here, too. It's just as strong. I bet when I come back to work here, I'll have the sensation wherever I am in the cemetery. I guess we can go home now that I know the feeling wasn't a one-time thing."

"Wait. There's a light on over there." Viv pointed.

Lin turned towards the cottage that the manager used as an office. A light was on at the back of the small house. "Quinn must be working late. He's the manager. Let's go. I don't want him to see me here."

The girls moved down the path to return to the truck and as they got closer to the middle of the path, Lin stopped and turned around slowly in a circle using the beam of the flashlight to illuminate the area around them.

"How do you feel?" Viv was ready to reach out her hand to steady her cousin.

"Dizzy still, but I'm getting used to the sensation. If I move slowly, then I feel steadier." Lin narrowed her eyes trying to make out anything at all that might be related to what was troubling her, but she didn't know what could be messing with her equilibrium. "Do you feel it at all?"

Viv's eyes went wide. "Me? No? And if I did, I would be *out* of here."

"It's strange. I've never felt anything like this before. It's almost like I can feel someone staring at me ... like someone wants something from me."

"You're scaring me." Viv looked up into the branches overhead afraid she might see someone up in the tree peering down at them. "I think I've had enough. Let's get out of here." She tugged on Lin's arm and the girls hurried to the truck like someone was after them.

Viv called for the animals and the two came scurrying out the woods and jumped into the cramped rear seat of the cab. Viv slammed the door, climbed into the passenger side, and slumped against the seat back. "So that was good for nothing." Her breath was quick and shallow.

"I'm glad we came." Lin looked through the windshield towards the woods. "Our visit told me that I didn't imagine the sensation from lunchtime and that I wasn't dizzy because I was dehydrated." She faced Viv. "And now I feel the sensation in the main part of the cemetery, too. It doesn't just feel like a ghost though. It feels like someone needs my help." Her heart pounded as she looked through the window at the dark woods. "What is it? Who's trying to communicate with me?"

CHAPTER 5

Lin tossed the last of the tools into the back of her truck and wiped the sweat from her brow with her forearm which left a streak of dirt on her head. It had been a long day working outside in the heat. She took a drink from her water bottle as she opened the door for the dog. Nicky jumped in and wagged his little stub of a tail.

"How are you still full of energy?" Lin smiled and scratched the dog's ears. "I need some of what you've got powering you."

The dog spent each day at work with Lin trotting about the clients' properties sniffing and searching the lawns and wooded areas discovering what animals had passed through since his last visit. Lin had trained him not to disturb flowers or greenery and he kept on his best behavior.

Lin stretched. "I need a long, hot shower." She also needed to make a potato salad and a green salad to take to Viv's house for dinner. The girls and their boyfriends had planned a cookout for later in the evening.

The mechanical rumble of an engine caused Lin to look to the road and she saw Leonard pull up to the curb. He leaned out of the window. "Hey, Coffin."

At the sound of Leonard's voice, Nicky jumped out of Lin's truck and he and Lin headed over to where the man had parked.

"I've got six extra rolls of sod in the back." He gestured with his thumb. "Why don't you take them for the Gordon's lawn. You said you wanted to replace some of the grass near their walkway." Leonard got out of the truck. "You've got dirt on your face."

Lin shrugged. "I've got dirt all over me."

The two removed the sod rolls and carried them to the bed of Lin's truck.

"I watered them this morning," Leonard said. "They'll be fine until you roll them out tomorrow."

"Any news on the farmhouse?" Lin pushed the last strip of sod into the truck bed.

"We don't have the all clear yet." Leonard leaned against the truck. "Hope they don't take forever investigating."

"What's the story with that house? What about the new owners?"

"The McDonalds haven't really even moved in yet. The house was for sale for a year. It was empty during that time. The couple has a few pieces of furniture in the house, but that's it."

"What are they like?"

"Young couple. Both docs. Anesthesiologists, I think. No kids. Once we finish the landscaping, they'll fly in most weekends from New York. The husband seems kind of uptight. He won't stay there for more than a couple of days until the yard is finished." Leonard chuckled. "He said he didn't like things in disarray. A chaotic setting was disturbing. Those were his words." Leonard gave Lin a questioning look. "You don't think they're to blame for the bone?"

Lin's shoulder shrugged. "Well, they own the house."

"They haven't for very long. Who knows how long that bone has been there?"

Lin didn't say anything.

"What?" Leonard raised an eyebrow. "You think when they make a medical mistake they bring the bones to Nantucket to dispose of them?"

"No, of course not," Lin said. "Well, unless they have a private plane."

Leonard was about to speak when Lin told him she was just joking. "But they could have killed someone while on-island. There are two of them. They're doctors. They must have medical instruments. The body gets cut up and they dispose of the parts here and there."

Leonard's eyes widened. "The McDonalds are anesthesiologists. They put people to sleep, they don't cut people up."

"They put people to sleep alright." Lin crossed

The Haunted Bones

her arms. "They're legitimate suspects."

"Unless the bone is old."

"If it *is* old, then I'll cross them off the list." Lin took two granola bars out of her cooler and handed one to Leonard. "I'd love to see what's going on at the farmhouse with the investigators." She peeled the wrapper back and took a bite.

"They won't let anyone near." Leonard chomped on the bar and chewed. While he was still chewing, he said, "There's a trail behind the house through the woods. It leads to a hill that might overlook the yard."

Lin perked up. "Really? How do you know?"

"My wife and I used to hike there a lot. It's conservation land ... for passive recreation."

"You think you could see into the yard from there?" Lin's voice was excited.

"I think so. I haven't been there for a couple of years though. It could be overgrown now, block out the view."

"Let's go look." Lin crumpled the granola wrapper and put it into the cooler. "Can you go now? Want to go see?"

Leonard agreed and they piled into his truck. They drove twenty minutes to the park and conservation area and the dog led the way down a winding trail through the woods.

"That dog can cover a lot of ground for a small fry," Leonard observed.

The trail began to incline and before long, they

were climbing a steep hill.

"Ugh." Sweat covered Lin's brow. "This isn't the most welcome climb after a hard day of work. Why aren't you puffing?"

"The real question is," Leonard said, "why are *you* puffing? I'm more than thirty years older than you, Coffin. Try to keep up."

After ten more minutes of uphill walking, they broke through the trees and entered a huge field.

"This is beautiful." Lin could see the ocean off in the distance on one side and on the other side, the rooftops of town peeked out between the trees.

Leonard pointed. "We might be able to see into the yards if we walk over that way." They headed to the left side of the field.

"Look." Lin's voice was excited. "There it is." The back of the farmhouse was in full view from their position on the hill. "The investigators are still working."

Several police officers stood around the space while other people, some in jumpsuits, milled about, took photos, or used tools to sift through the dirt. A leashed dog, his nose to the ground, moved back and forth over the rear yard.

"Cadaver dog?" Leonard speculated.

Nicky gave a whine when he spotted the other creature.

"I didn't realize that all these people would be involved." Lin watched the activity below them.

"If they find more bones, it might be a while

before we can get that project underway."

"If they find more bones...." Lin said warily. She sank down and sat on the grass. "What will that mean? Is there a murderer on the loose?" She looked up at Leonard. "Is there someone who has gone missing on the island?"

"That I don't know." Leonard continued to follow the activity in the yard.

Lin's mind was racing. "You said the farmhouse was empty for about a year?"

"Uh, huh. That's what the McDonalds told me."

"An empty house. A lot can happen in a year with no one around."

"What do you mean?"

"No one was keeping tabs on the place. Well, maybe a Realtor came by once a week or a property manager or whatever. But that's a good amount of time that the house was just sitting there." Lin made eye contact with Leonard. "Someone who had no business there could have gone by, lurked around the back of the property. Maybe buried some bones."

"You've got a point."

Nicky barked and Lin turned to see a woman walking with a yellow Lab in the field behind them. "Stay here, Nick." The woman waved and Lin returned the gesture of greeting.

Lin stood and glanced around wondering if the farmhouse's neighbors might have noticed anything during the time the house was vacant. The trees surrounding the place made it difficult for the people living next door to see the back of the property but, in the winter when the branches were bare, there might be decent visibility from house to house. A skitter of anxiety washed over Lin remembering the odd feeling she had when Nicky found the bone. "I wonder if the neighbors would be willing to talk to me."

Leonard gave her the eye. "Why would you want to talk to the neighbors? The police must have talked to them. We don't have any business asking questions."

"I found the bone."

"You aren't an investigator." Leonard ran his hand over his hair. "Best leave it to the police."

Lin sighed. She recalled the feeling she had when Emily Coffin made eye contact with her the other evening when Nicky uncovered the bone. Standing at the edge of the field with Leonard, her fingers could almost feel the little sparks that had picked at her hand when she held it.

Lin knew why Emily was watching. Emily wanted her to get involved. But she also knew that there was a reason to investigate that was even more important than that.

The bone wanted Lin to get involved.

CHAPTER 6

After watching the yard of the farmhouse, Leonard dropped Lin off to pick up her truck and she and Nicky headed to one last stop. She wanted to replace some flowers at the cemetery entrance that weren't holding up well in the summer heat. Driving along, Lin kept the window down so the breeze would rush in through the opening and cool her.

Thinking about what they'd seen from their perch on the hill, Lin couldn't stop contemplating the bone, how it got in that yard, and who it belonged to. She was so deep in thought that she almost missed the turn to the cemetery. Glancing at the dashboard clock, she realized she had to hurry with the planting so she could get home in time to make the salads for the cookout.

Pulling past the old wrought-iron gates, Lin parked as far to the left as she could so as not to block the entrance. Her truck's engine sputtered and coughed and turned off. She lifted the new flowers and some tools out of the truck and with the dog at her side, she went to work on removing the old blooms and replacing them.

A man's voice called her name and she turned to see the cemetery manager, Quinn Whitaker, walking over to her. "How are things? That truck of yours doesn't sound too good."

Lin stood. "I'm afraid it's on its way out. It doesn't always want to start up in the mornings." The two exchanged some pleasantries.

Quinn said, "The place looks great. You're doing good work."

"The summer's been so hot, it's taking a toll on some of the flowers. I'm taking a few annuals out and replacing them." She pointed at the flower bed.

"I appreciate it." Quinn nodded. "You're keeping things looking fresh." He checked his watch. "I just got back from the mainland this morning. Work is backed up now because I was away, so I'll be staying late tonight."

"You took some time off?" Lin brushed some dirt from her hands. She hoped Quinn wasn't going to chat much longer. She needed to put these flowers in so she could get home.

"Just a few days. I had to tend to some family things," Quinn said. "Elderly issues."

Even though she'd never had the responsibility of aging parents, Lin gave a nod. Her parents had died when she little and her grandfather had raised her. He passed away a few months ago and left Lin the cottage.

The Haunted Bones

While Quinn made a few more comments about the weather and the work he was behind on, something picked at Lin's brain. Quinn headed back to work and Lin bent to finish up the plantings when what she'd been puzzling over popped into her mind. She looked over her shoulder and called to Quinn. "Is the office light on a timer?"

Quinn stopped walking and faced Lin. He cocked his head. "No, why?"

"I came back late last night." Realizing she had to explain why she had been at the cemetery at night, she made something up. "I left one of my new tools here and I didn't want to lose it, so I came back to get it. There was a light on in the back room." She gestured toward the back of the office cottage. "I thought you were working late. It must have been one of the employees."

Quinn seemed surprised. He looked over at the cottage, then turned back to Lin and smiled. "No one else has a key. It must have been the moon shining on the window."

Lin was about to say that she didn't think it could have been the moonlight, but Quinn spoke before she said so. "No one was here at night." He waved and headed back inside.

Holding a trowel in one hand, Lin sat back on her heels. *I know there was a light on in there. If it wasn't Quinn, then who was it?*

***

Lin scurried around making the salads, showering and dressing so she wouldn't be late to dinner. She and Nicky hurried along the brick walkways that lined the cobbled streets to Lin's house. Roses and hydrangeas bloomed in Viv's gardens inside the white picket fence that enclosed the front yard. Lin got a whiff of the roses as she walked down the driveway to the back of the house and the deck. She could hear Jeff and John talking and when she came around the corner, she saw them standing by the grill.

Jeff took the platters from his girlfriend and kissed her. "You look great." His eyes shined.

"Viv's inside." John lifted the lid of the grill to check the charcoals. "We can put the food on in a minute."

Jeff, Viv, and Lin carried food and drinks out to the deck and John placed burgers, shish kebobs, and skewers of vegetables onto the grill. Nicky and Queenie dozed in the grass under one of the trees.

Lin told everyone about how she and Leonard climbed the hill at the park and came out right above the farmhouse's backyard. She described the scene of police and officials as they scoured the rear of the house looking for additional bones.

Jeff put his arm around Lin's shoulders. "I hope it's an old bone from decades ago."

Viv agreed. "There's been enough excitement on the island this summer. If this keeps up, they'll change the name to Murder Island."

Lin groaned.

John flipped a burger. "It sounds strange, but that would probably bring even more tourists over from the mainland. Plenty of people like murder mysteries and intrigue." He looked up pondering. "Maybe it would do my business good. How could I capitalize on that?"

Viv bopped John's arm playfully. "Honestly John, you can't try to profit off someone else's misery."

"Leonard told me that the farmhouse was for sale for almost year," Lin said.

"Yeah. I really wanted to sell that place." John checked the grilling vegetables. "I just missed out on taking the call from those doctors who ended up buying it."

Lin held a platter for John to place the skewers. "When a place for sale is empty, do Realtors make some arrangements to have the house and property checked on periodically?"

"Some do." John placed the veggies and burgers on the platter. "Our firm does. There's a risk of a squatter moving in especially in the off-season or there could be other trouble like kids getting inside and destroying the place. There was a multimillion dollar house in Cisco that was closed up for the winter. Teens got in and trashed it, turned the water on which burst all the pipes. It was a mess, to say the least. It took tens of thousands of dollars to fix it."

"So at your firm, does the listing Realtor check on the house or do you hire someone to go by?" Lin handed the food platter to Jeff and he carried it to the deck.

"Both. We try to have someone check the house at least twice a week. We do it at random times in case anyone is watching for patterns. It usually works pretty well."

"Why all the questions?" Viv gave Lin a wary look while she lit the candles on the deck table. She wondered what her cousin might have in mind to drag her into.

Lin said, "I wonder about the bone. How did it get in the ground behind the farmhouse?"

"That bone is probably ancient." Viv walked down the deck steps and put her arms around John from behind. "And if it is ancient, then it doesn't matter how it got there."

"If it's an old bone, it would be nearly impossible to figure out the circumstances that brought it to the farmhouse yard." Jeff handed tongs to John so he could take the shish kebob skewers off the grill.

When the platter was full, the four young people sat at the table and dug into the food. The smell of the meal made everyone's mouths water.

"Delicious," Jeff pronounced.

Conversation turned to other things besides a discovered bone and the dinner was devoured. The yard darkened as the sun set and the four people sat sipping drinks and watching fireflies dart about in the night. John suggested some music and he and Jeff cleared away the plates and went inside to get Viv's guitars.

Lin leaned close to her cousin. "My last stop today was the cemetery. I talked to Quinn Whitaker, the manager. It was strange. He said he'd been off-island for a few days."

Viv raised an eyebrow in question. "And?"

"When you and I went to the cemetery last night there was a light on in one of the office back rooms. You saw it."

"Yeah, I remember. You didn't want the manager to see us there so late."

Lin nodded. "Quinn said he wasn't at the cemetery last night. He went to the mainland for a few days to take care of some family responsibility."

Viv sipped some water. "There must be a timer on the light then."

"I said that to him. He told me there was no timer. He said it must have been the moonlight reflecting off the window glass." A cloud seemed to have settled over Lin's expression. "Quinn told me that he's the only one who has a key to the office."

"He didn't say that things were missing from the office?" A shadow of concern flitted over Viv's face.

"He acted like everything was normal." Lin glanced around the dark yard, thinking. She could hear the guys returning to the deck with the musical instruments. She whispered to her cousin. "Someone was in that office."

Viv made eye contact with Lin. "I wonder who it was."

"And...." Lin frowned. "What was the person doing in there?"

CHAPTER 7

Lin stopped at Viv's bookstore before heading off to her first gardening client of the day. Nicky pranced in and trotted right to the chair where Queenie always sat. The gray cat lifted her regal head from her paw when the little dog zoomed over and put his front paws on the chair. She slid closer to the upholstered armrest to make room for him and he leaped up, slurped her cheek and settled down next to her. Queenie raised a paw, licked it, and wiped at the spot where the dog had planted the kiss.

Lin looked around the café section of the bookstore at the patrons sitting at tables and on sofas enjoying their morning beverages and treats. She saw Viv behind the counter waiting on someone and she gave her cousin a smile. As she turned back, Libby Hartnett, an older island native, made eye contact with Lin. Lin nodded, and Libby said something to her companions and stood up.

Lin walked to a table and Libby joined her.

Libby had silvery-white hair that was cut short and was feathered around her face. Her blue eyes were striking in their intensity. Libby had been friendly with Lin's grandfather and Libby and Lin were distant relatives descended from the Witchard family, a family where many of the women had some kind of powers. Lin guessed that Libby might be in her seventies, but it was only a guess, and the older woman certainly wasn't about to be forthcoming on the subject.

"You want to talk?" Libby sat and placed her mug of coffee on the table. She sensed that Lin needed to discuss something just by seeing the expression on her face when she came into the store.

"Have you seen the news story about the bone that was found?" Lin folded her arms on the tabletop.

"I did." Libby gave a slight nod never moving her eyes from the young woman's face.

Lin's shoulders drooped. "I was the one who found it."

Libby sat up straight, her eyes wide.

"Emily Coffin was there, too."

Libby tilted her head slightly to the side. "Did she communicate with you?"

A cloud settled over Lin's face. From time to time, ghosts appeared to her, but they never spoke. A few months ago, Lin thought that Sebastian Coffin might be trying to say something to her. It felt like a message was hanging on the air between them, yet it just floated there, the words and meaning never fully forming.

"Tell me what happened." Libby listened closely as Lin told her about Nicky digging in the pile of dirt behind the farmhouse and discovering the bone. She also reported her odd feelings while on the trail and in the cemetery.

"Your sensations are probably related to the discovery of the bone." Libby tapped her manicured finger against her chin. "Stay aware. Be open to any messages that a spirit might try to send to you. Just because they haven't communicated in the past doesn't mean they won't in the future." Libby lowered her voice. "Messages can come through without words so pay attention to things you think are your own thoughts or intuitions. I've known other people who can see ghosts. They don't receive audible messages. It's more like a silent communication, hearing the message in your mind. So be aware of that possibility during a visitation."

Lin almost cringed at the word *visitation*. She thought it sounded weird and creepy.

Libby's face was serious. "Be on guard, listen to your intuition."

"Do you know who the previous owners of the farmhouse were?" Lin wondered if Libby might have any information that might shed some light on the recent happenings.

"My friend owned that house for ages." Libby looked wistful. "When she passed away, it was sold to a man who only kept it for two years. The place was on the market for some time until only recently when it was sold again."

"A couple of doctors bought the place. Leonard and I have contracted with them to do the landscaping." Lin traced a crack in the tabletop with her fingertip. "Have you heard anything about the bone? Is it old? How did it end up behind the farmhouse?"

Libby shook her head. "Nothing has been reported yet."

"Why do I keep thinking about this bone?" Lin rubbed her forehead. "Oh, I know Emily Coffin wants me to look into it, but what can I do? The police have the bone. They have the means to figure out how old it is. They're the ones with the labs and the techs and the research tools."

Libby stared at Lin for a few moments. "But you're the one with the ghosts."

Lin blew out a long breath and narrowed her eyes. "They're not all that much help."

"Maybe you need to listen more closely."

Lin sighed.

"Like I said, there's more than one way to hear something." Libby patted Lin's hand. "You'll get better at it."

Lin was about to ask more questions when one of Libby's morning coffee buddies walked up to the table to chat. After several minutes, Libby checked her watch and stood up. "I need to get to work." The woman worked part time at a high-end home goods shop in Nantucket town. She leaned down. "Talk to the neighbors. See if that leads anywhere."

Lin thought over what she and Libby talked about. After a few minutes, she collected the dog, chatted with Viv for a few minutes, and headed out the door to her truck feeling as confused and unsure of how to investigate the bone as when she arrived. Stepping onto the sidewalk, she nearly collided with Viv's boyfriend. They chuckled at their almost head-on crash.

"Did you stop in for coffee or just to see Viv?" John asked.

"I was planning to have coffee, but I realized I have some extra gardens to work on today so I couldn't stay." Lin couldn't tell John that she'd come by to talk to Libby Hartnett about the bone ... and ghosts.

John was about to go into the bookstore when he stopped and faced Lin. He took a step closer and glanced up and down the sidewalk. "You know I have a friend at the police station? He told me that the bone you found is probably male. They don't know how long it's been in that yard or how it got there. He also said that no other bones were found on the farmhouse property, so that's good news. You and Leonard can start on the job there soon."

Lin took a step closer. "Did your friend say anything else? Is the bone old or did it come from someone recently deceased?"

"It's not new, but an exact age wasn't

determined. That's all he told me."

Lin thanked John for the information and was about to walk to her truck when John asked something. "I have a house showing later today, at 8pm. Viv can't get away." John shuffled his feet and glanced down at the brick sidewalk.

Lin was confused for a few seconds and then it dawned on her why John was bringing up the showing. "You want me to go along?"

"The house is empty." John gave a shrug of one shoulder and his cheeks looked flushed. He was still having trouble showing a house to prospective buyers when the place was unoccupied since he'd discovered a murder victim at an empty house last month. "I'm still working on getting over going into an empty house." He gave Lin a sad smile.

"I'll go along. Nicky will come, too." Lin looked down at her dog and smiled.

Looking at the small creature, John said, "That's all the protection we'll need." He chuckled. "I feel better already."

Nicky woofed.

Lin started up the street to where her truck was parked. "Small doesn't mean weak, you know," she called over her shoulder. "Remember, this dog helped protect me from an attacker two months ago. You could do a whole lot worse for a bodyguard than this little guy." Lin and the dog got into the truck and Lin leaned out the window. "Text me the address later and we'll meet you at the showing."

Turning the key in the ignition, some words she'd said to John stuck in her head and kept repeating. *Bodyguard. Bodyguard.*

What about it?

CHAPTER 8

Lin met Leonard at the farmhouse at lunchtime to have a look at the back of the property to see what the investigators did to the area while digging for any new bones. They thought the additional disruption to the yard might require some tweaking to their work plan.

"Looks okay." Leonard gazed at the dirt piles. "It'll just need some extra work with the front loader." He gave Lin a grin. "You must be happy about that."

The two went over the documents showing the landscape designs, pointed out some things that needed adjustment, and made their plan for the following days. Leonard headed off to another job while Lin stood at her truck rolling up the paperwork. Putting it on the backseat, she glanced over to the neighbor's house. It could barely be seen through the lush greenery. Lin decided that this was as good a time as any, so she and the dog cut through the trees and bushes and came out on the neighbor's crushed shell driveway. Taking a deep breath she went to the front of the three-story home and rang the bell.

It only took a few seconds for the door to open. A woman in her early sixties with chin-length auburn hair stood at the entrance smiling at Lin. "Hi, there. Can I help with something?"

Lin introduced herself and explained that she and her partner would be working in the rear yard next door. "Since no one's usually at the house, I just wanted you to know that we'd be coming and going."

A tall, strong-looking man came up behind the woman. He also looked to be in his sixties and had salt and pepper hair and deep-set dark eyes. His thick eyebrows were like two caterpillars placed on his forehead. They scrunched together in a concerned expression. "You're not removing any of the trees or bushes that line the edge of the property, are you?"

"Not at all." Lin reassured the man. "The couple who owns the house want to keep the vegetation along the property line. We'll just be working along the edges of the area creating new flower beds. It won't impact you at all."

The man scowled. "I'm sure the noise you'll be making will impact us."

"Oh, Lloyd, honestly." The woman shook her head. "Everyone has work done on their places now and then."

Lin said, "We'll be working within the hours of

eight to five in order to keep the noise down. We'll only be using a small front loader on the first two days of the job. Then everything will just be some trucks arriving and manual labor."

The woman held out her hand. "I'm Olive Sawyer. This is my husband, Lloyd."

The man didn't offer to shake hands, just gave Lin a curt nod.

"There's already been a lot going on next door the past few days." Lin was leading up to asking the couple about things they'd seen over the past year. "It was an unfortunate find."

"You found that bone, didn't you?" Lloyd was almost accusatory.

Lin's eyebrows shot up in surprise and she nodded. She remembered seeing a man on the other side of the trees that night and realized it must have been Lloyd. "My partner and I were reviewing the landscaping plans the other evening. My dog was the one who discovered the bone."

"How terrible to find such a thing." Olive wrapped her arms around herself. "I'm so glad they didn't find any more bones." She gave a shudder.

"I wonder how it got there." Lin looked at Olive hoping that the woman might share some speculation.

"I wish we knew." Olive's lips were pulled down.

Lin said, "The farmhouse was empty for a year, I heard. I guess someone could have accessed the yard during that time."

The Haunted Bones

"We aren't here in the winter. We close up for the cold weather and head home to New York City." Olive's voice took on a concerned tone. "I did see people back there once in a while though."

Lloyd cut in. "That was the Realtor checking on the property." He gave Lin a look. "My wife likes to ignore the humdrum explanation."

"Things aren't always as they seem." Olive faced Lin. "When no one is living in a house, there's a chance that someone might break in and cause trouble. There's nothing wrong with keeping an eye on the place. It's the neighborly thing to do."

"Who lived there before the new couple bought it?" Lin questioned.

Olive said, "George Lyons, a business owner, owned the place. I don't know why he wanted it."

Lloyd cut into the conversation. "The man used it as an investment."

Olive clucked. "A home should be lived in. Lyons hardly ever used the place. The first year, he might have been there for a total of four weekends, but the rest of the time, the house was empty. The second year, he put it up for rent. After that, he put the place up for sale."

"What were the rental people like? Did someone rent it for a full year?"

"No." Lloyd scowled again and Lin wondered if that was his usual expression. She felt badly for Olive having to live with such a sour puss. "A family rented it for the summer. So much noise over there, a bunch of kids always shouting in the backyard."

Olive made a face at her husband's comments. "I liked it. The yard was full of life. In the off-season, a writer and her husband rented it September through March. Then a single man took over for April and May." She scrunched up her nose. "I didn't care for him."

"Then that family brought their noise back with them in the summer." Lloyd grunted. "I have to get back to work." He turned abruptly and moved down the hallway with heavy steps.

Lin watched him go and then looked at Olive with a friendly expression. She hoped that the woman would continue their conversation for a bit longer.

"Don't mind, Lloyd." Olive waved her hand in his direction. "He's an old fuss-budget. He has a very rigid way of thinking about the world."

Lin wanted to ask Olive how on earth she could stand living with him, but thought better of it.

Olive nodded to the house next door. "The house just sat idle for almost the whole year while it was up for sale."

Lin said, "I wonder why George Lyons didn't rent the house that last year."

Olive gave a shrug. "He probably thought it would sell quickly and didn't want to have a rental agreement to honor that might slow the sale. He probably just wanted to unload the place."

"Did you ever see any suspicious activity next door?" So far the conversation wasn't shedding any light on how the bone might have ended up in the farmhouse's backyard. "Somebody lurking who didn't belong there? Lights on when they weren't supposed to be?"

Olive shook her head. "I'd see somebody walking around the house, but Lloyd always said it was the real estate agent or a property manager checking up on it." She laughed. "I *was* ready to call the police one night though. I saw the light of a flashlight in the yard, but it turned out to be Lloyd."

Lin's eyes narrowed. "Lloyd was over there?"

Olive smiled. "Imagine the police showing up and it's my own husband that I called in about."

"Why was Lloyd in the backyard?"

"He said he thought he heard someone over there ... he thought he saw a light in the yard."

Lin cocked her head. "He wasn't concerned for his safety? If it was an intruder?"

Olive batted the air with her hand. "Lloyd does things in his own way."

Lin wondered what else Lloyd might do in his own way. She forced a smile. "When did that happen?"

"Oh, months ago."

They talked for a few more minutes and then Lin thanked her for her time and started down the front steps. Thinking of something, she stopped. "You mentioned you didn't like the man who rented the farmhouse in April and May. What bothered you about him?"

Olive's expression darkened. "He was unfriendly, abrupt. I went over with some cookies to welcome him and he just poked his head out of the door. He only opened it a crack, like he was trying to hide something. He gave me a bad feeling."

Lin waited to see if she might add to her comments, but the woman had a faraway look on her face and didn't say any more. "Thank you for talking with me," Lin said.

"You know," Olive said slowly.

Lin made eye contact with her.

"I thought I saw that guy in the yard after he'd moved out." Olive gestured to the farmhouse. "It was dark, but there was a security light that lit up part of the yard. The guy walked briefly under the light. I thought it looked just like him." She shook her head. "Lloyd said it was just my imagination running away with me."

"What did you think of Lloyd's explanation?"

Olive was quiet for a few seconds and then her jaw seemed to tighten. The woman leveled her eyes at Lin. "I thought he was wrong."

CHAPTER 9

Driving to meet John at the house showing, Lin couldn't stop thinking about her visit to the farmhouse neighbors. Olive seemed to believe that she saw the creepy renter guy behind the farmhouse at night at a time when he wasn't even renting and she reported that Lloyd was skulking around back there in the dark one night claiming to have heard and seen a possible intruder. Lin's mind was replaying the events that had happened over the past few days and it all seemed like a carousel that was spinning faster and faster making everything a blur.

She pulled to the curb of a long driveway and she and the dog got out. In the gathering dusk, Lin could see John's car parked at the end of the driveway near the house. The vehicle's interior overhead light was on and she could make out John's head bent forward. When she reached the side of the car, Lin could see that John was going over some paperwork. She said his name and waved at his window which caused John's head to snap up as he whirled towards the sound.

When John saw Lin, he blew out a long breath. He opened the driver side door and stepped out. "I didn't hear you come up. I'm feeling jumpy."

Nicky gave the man a soft woof and wagged his little tail. John bent to scratch his ears.

"It's okay." Lin gave John's arm a quick squeeze. "Being nervous will pass. You just need to give it time. You should make these appointments in the daylight until you feel better about going into unoccupied houses." She looked over at the building. "It looks pretty run down."

"It is. It's a mess." John locked his car and removed the house key from his briefcase. "The price is right for a person who has some money to put into renovations. Doing renovations could double or triple the value of the place." John led the way to the front door.

"Can Nicky come in with us?"

"He *is* my bodyguard," John joked as he pushed open the door.

John's words caused a slight shiver to travel over Lin's skin and not knowing why she had that reaction, she gave herself a shake trying to throw off the strange unease.

The house was dark and musty. The tiles in the entryway were cracked and loose. Dingy wallpaper covered the foyer walls. John fumbled for the light switch and flicked it on illuminating the living room.

The Haunted Bones

Lin glanced around the sad room's disrepair. The wood floors were scuffed and stained and a few pieces of old, torn upholstered furniture stood haphazardly about the space. The window glass was covered in grime.

John groaned. "The guy from the office was supposed to come and remove this furniture."

Lin looked at him, the corner of her mouth turning up. "The furniture isn't going to be the thing that stops the sale of this place."

"It just makes it look worse." Pulling out his phone, John made a call to the office. He paced back and forth as he talked.

Lin walked around and entered what was once used as a dining room. It was in the same sorry state as the living area. Lin leaned down near the window and peering through the grimy streaks, tried to look out into the darkening yard. She straightened up with a start. Emily Coffin stood in the side yard staring up at Lin. Her ghostly body shimmered in the evening light.

Lin bit her lower lip, her mind racing. *Why is she here? What does it mean?* Her heart sank. She walked back into the living room where John was still pacing and talking into the phone. He glanced up at Lin and she mouthed, *I'm going to go look around.*

John nodded.

"Come on, Nick." Lin led the way to the other rooms with the dog right at her heels. Tension gathered in her muscles and she consciously tried to relax and release them. She reached to her throat for her gold pendant with the horseshoe on it. While she moved her index finger over the edges of the necklace, she tried to slow her breathing and calm her pounding heart. She was sure there was something in the house that Emily Coffin wanted her to find. *Where is it? What is it?*

On the first floor and then on the second, Lin moved from room to room, holding her breath as she flicked on the lights and opened the closet doors. Relief flooded her body each time a space was empty. Despite her attempts to control it, her tension was making her feel shaky. "I guess the coast is clear, Nick." She and the dog hurried down the staircase. John stood in the living room sending text messages. He looked up when Lin came in.

"The clients are late. They called when you were upstairs. They'll be here in about fifteen minutes." John looked hopefully at Lin. "Can you stay?"

"Sure. It's fine." Lin nodded, but what she really wanted was to rush from the empty house and run to her car. She needed to get control of her nerves.

"I'm going to run out to the car to get some paperwork." John went out the front door.

From the other room, Nicky let out a long whine that sent a shudder though Lin's body. She turned and walked into the kitchen to find the dog. The little brown creature sat in front of a door. He lifted his foot and pawed at it. Lin glanced over her shoulder to the living room and then flicked her gaze back to the door. She wanted to call to John to have him come into the kitchen, but if something unpleasant was behind the door, she didn't want to add another distressing find to his current anxious state. Lin considered telling John that they needed to leave the building, but she pushed the idea out of her head.

Nicky pawed the door again and whined.

Lin blew out a breath and put her hand on the door knob. She turned it slowly and squeezed her eyes into slits so she would have only partial sight. She pulled the door open to find the stairs to the basement.

Lin looked down the stairs into the dingy cellar and then shifted her eyes to the dog. "No way I'm going down there."

Before Lin could grab him, Nicky rushed down the steps into the basement and disappeared around the corner.

Lin almost stomped her foot in frustration. She called to the dog. He wouldn't return. Reaching for the light switch, she pushed on the button to turn the cellar lights on. Hesitating, Lin put her hand on the side of her face and closed her eyes for a few seconds. Opening them again, she sucked in a deep breath, grabbed the rickety banister, and slow step by slow step, descended into the cellar.

***

Lin reached the bottom of the stairs and warily looked around the basement. An old wooden work bench stood to one side. Two by fours were strewn across the floor, used paint cans were stacked in rows on the left side of the space, there was a box holding some rotted fire wood, and a couple of broken chairs lay in a heap.

"Nicky." Lin's voice was stern. She wanted to find the dog and get out of there.

Lin heard something scratch on the floor. She edged around the corner into a smaller space that had a dirt floor. Lin fumbled along the wall trying to find a light switch. She let out an exasperated sigh when her fingers couldn't locate it. Squinting into the dank space, she made out the form of the dog. He whined sending a shiver down her spine.

"What are you doing, Nick?" Lin moved her feet a few inches at a time as she shuffled closer. The dog sat next to a rusty locker that lay on the floor like it had fallen from its upright position and was left there by someone who thought it was more useful that way. Nicky pawed the metal.

Lin's throat tightened as if fingers were laced around her neck. A wave of dizziness came over her and she reached her hand out to find something to steady herself. Her fingers floundered in the air so she slowly sank onto her knees and put her hand on top of the locker. Zings of electricity nipped at her fingers and she yanked her arm back.

Lin's heart pounded like it was going to leap from her chest. When the dizziness passed, she moved her trembling hand to the handle on the locker. Terrified of what she might find, she steeled herself and sucked in a breath. Twisting the knob, she flung the metal door open.

Lin's feet scurried under her so quickly in a scramble to get away that she toppled onto her back with a heavy thud.

A sound hurt her ears. She realized it was the sound of her own scream.

CHAPTER 10

Lin rolled onto her side and then to her hands and knees. She crawled back to the metal locker and, holding her breath, peered inside for a second time. At the bottom of the shallow locker lay a partial skeleton. The eye sockets of the skull seemed like dark eyes staring at Lin. Shaking off the shock of her find, Lin sat down on the dirt floor. Nicky licked her cheek.

"Lin!" John's voice called from upstairs. His feet pounded the treads of the staircase as he descended into the basement.

Lin clambered to her feet and rushed into the main part of the basement. "I'm okay." Knowing that her discovery would only add to John's anxiety of finding a dead body in a house last month, she didn't want John to see the skeleton without first warning him about it. "I got startled by something."

John stared at the obviously shaken young woman. "What was it? What's wrong?"

Lin's hand trembled as she pushed her hair away

from her forehead. "I found another bone. A skull actually."

John looked like he'd been slapped. "A skull? Where?" His voice seemed higher than normal and his eyes darted about the cellar.

"Let's go upstairs." Lin took John's arm and tugged. "You don't need to see it. We have to call the police."

John hesitated, but then allowed Lin to lead him to the staircase. They climbed the steps to the kitchen and went into the living room where Lin was about to sink onto one of the ratty upholstered chairs, but then thought better of it. Her body was shaking slightly from the adrenaline rush that had surged through her veins. Glancing around for a place to sit, she slid to the floor with her back against the wall.

"Can I use your phone?" she asked John.

He handed it to her.

The sound of a car door slamming caused John to turn to the front door and then immediately back to Lin. "The clients."

Lin shook her head as she pushed the police emergency number into the phone. She tried to kid, "Just don't let them go into the basement." When the dispatcher answered Lin's call, she reported the address and said, "I found a partial skeleton in the basement."

John's eyes went wide and his voice almost squeaked. "I thought it was just a skull."

As Lin clicked off from the call, she raised an eyebrow at John wondering why only a skull would be less worrisome than a partial skeleton. "It's a little more than a skull."

John's face was so white and his posture so stooped that Lin wondered if he would ever be able to show another house again. Lin pushed herself off the floor and headed to the door with John and Nicky right behind her. They stepped outside to wait for the police.

"You might want to tell your clients that this isn't really a good time."

John groaned and rolled his eyes. "The understatement of the week."

***

When the police arrived, John and Lin were questioned and the house and basement were searched. Viv arrived to provide support and Jeff, who was on the mainland for a couple of days, talked to Lin by phone. After two hours, the police told them they were free to go. Despite Viv's near insistence that John come to her house to relax, he decided to head to his office to catch up on paperwork. With a sigh and a shake of her head, Viv got into her car and followed Lin to her house.

Once in the kitchen, Lin put the kettle on and Viv poured a glass of wine. "Tea just isn't going to cut it for me." Lin could see her cousin's hand shaking slightly as she raised the glass to her lips.

"Is John okay?" Lin poured hot water into her tea cup. "He's had some tough encounters lately."

"He'll be okay. John's a sweet softy, but he won't let these things interfere with his life." Viv pushed a strand of her hair behind her ear. "At least today he didn't *see* the skeleton. He's trying to work through his anxiety from finding that dead body. It will take time. I'll keep my eye on him though."

The girls took seats in the comfy chairs in the living room. Nicky jumped on the sofa and was asleep in a few seconds. Lin looked at him and smiled. "I'm exhausted, too." Her body felt weak from the after effects of the adrenaline rush.

"What is going on around here?" Viv asked. "What's with all these bones showing up?"

"Do you think the partial skeleton and the leg bone found at the farmhouse go together?" Lin questioned.

A horrified look washed over Viv's face. "I didn't think of that. Ugh. Why would the parts be separated?"

"We need to find out if the bones belong to one person or two people." Lin pulled a cashmere throw blanket over her knees.

"Why does that matter?" Viv looked a bit pale.

"Because, if it's two people then we have a bigger problem than we thought." Lin put her elbow on the arm of the chair and rested her chin in her hand. "And, if the bones belong to two different people, then I would make a bet that there are more bones hidden out there from other people."

Viv stood up and wrapped her arms around her body. She started to pace about the room. "Why is this happening?" She glanced at the door to the deck, hurried over and checked to see that it was locked. Viv strode into the kitchen, opened a drawer, and returned to the living room carrying a small boning knife.

A grin spread over Lin's face. "No one is after us."

"I'm not taking any chances." Viv sat down and took a swallow of her wine. She stood up again and flicked the wall switch to illuminate the back deck. "I don't want anyone sneaking up to the windows and looking in at us."

"Emily Coffin was at the house." Lin held her tea cup in her hand.

Viv stared wide-eyed at Lin. "Did she say anything? Was it Emily who led you to the skeleton?"

Lin sighed. "You know the ghosts never say a word to me. I looked out the window of the dining room and there she was, standing outside in the dark. She made eye contact with me. I knew something must be in the house, but I thought it might be a clue about the bone from the farmhouse." Lin's forehead creased in thought. "Maybe this skeleton *is* a clue." She looked at her cousin. "How are we going to figure this out?

There's hardly anything to go on."

"John's friend at the police station can probably give him some information." Viv slid to the edge of her seat. "It isn't much that he hears, but it's something. Maybe the news stories will have some important information that will help."

Lin nodded. "Anything can help. I need to think over what we know."

Viv wrinkled her nose. "From what you've told me, that Lloyd guy seems like an odd ball. His wife saw him in the yard of the farmhouse one night. That seems weird, doesn't it?"

Lin nodded. "He seemed the type who wouldn't go sneaking around if he thought someone was trespassing at the farmhouse. He'd call the police and let them handle it." Lin rubbed her shoulder. "I only met him briefly, though, so who knows what he's really like."

"And his wife, Olive, she thinks a former renter was in the back of the farmhouse months after he moved out. That's suspicious, too."

Lin frowned. "But Lloyd said Olive was mistaken. It was just someone checking on the house." Lin sat up. "I wonder if John can tell us the name of the person who rented the house, the guy Olive thinks was lurking in the yard. Maybe he's still on-island and I could go and talk to him. See what he's like. Ask if he ever noticed anyone in the yard while he was renting."

"Good idea."

Lin's eyes widened. "The Mid-Island Cemetery."

Viv looked at her cousin. "What about it?"

"Someone was in the office the night we were there. Quinn says he was on the mainland at the time and that no one else has a key to the office." Lin's eyes darkened. "Someone was in there."

"What would be the reason for being in there? There wasn't anything missing or Quinn would have realized that there was a break-in. Why would anyone want to break into a cemetery office?" Viv huddled back in her chair.

Lin sighed. "I'm going to make more tea. Want some more wine?"

Viv held her glass out. "Or just bring me the whole bottle," she kidded.

Lin started for the kitchen. "You can probably put that knife down on the side table."

Viv still clutched the weapon in her hand. She considered, and then reluctantly placed the knife on the small table next to her chair.

Lin smiled. "Like I said, I think we're safe. It's just dead people that someone is after." Lin halted in her tracks. She turned slowly to her cousin and the look on her face gave Viv a start.

"What's wrong with you?" Viv's voice shook.

"Dead people. Bones." Lin's eyes were like lasers. "Grave robbers."

CHAPTER 11

"Grave robbers?" Viv gave Lin a skeptical look. "What does that even mean? Why would someone rob a grave?"

"I read about this happening on the mainland, in central Massachusetts, not too long ago." Lin came back into the living room forgetting about getting another cup of tea. "A group of people, well, the story I read about had three people involved, robbed graves and mausoleums to sell the bodies."

Viv's jaw dropped. "Sell them to who? How much money could someone get for a body?"

"There are a few different markets." Lin sat down on the ottoman next to Viv. "The bones get sold to third party marketers and then they distribute the bodies or bones to legitimate sellers."

"What on earth is a legitimate seller?" Viv had her hand on her throat. "Wait, maybe I don't want to know."

Lin leaned forward. "A legitimate seller is a business broker that gets bodies or bones and sells them to universities, medical schools, body farms, or even private buyers."

Viv looked like she'd tasted something sour. "I know I shouldn't ask this because I don't really want to know the answer, but what is a body farm?"

Lin tried to choose her words carefully. "It's a research lab. Outside. Scientists study decomposition to help understand forensics in order to aid in investigations. It helps in training forensic anthropologists, detectives, medical examiners."

"Well." Viv tried not to sound alarmed by this bit of information.

"Of course, that's not what we're dealing with in this case. We just have bones. Someone might be selling them to brokers." Lin reached for Viv's nearly empty wine glass and took a sip. "Some people rob graves looking for valuables like rings, bracelets, necklaces to sell off. I've read that some graves have been robbed to hold the body until the family pays a ransom to get it back."

"How awful." Viv leaned back in her chair. "Are you making this up?"

"You can look it all up on the internet. That's where I read about it."

"I can't believe this." Viv shook her head not wanting to accept that something so ghoulish was happening on her island.

"Who knows the reason someone would be doing this here?" Lin looked at her cousin. "But it's a possibility. Why would a skeleton be in the basement of that house? Why would the bone be in the ground behind the farmhouse? Grave robbing makes sense. The bones have been found at houses that are unoccupied. It would be easy to hide a body or some bones on the property of an empty house. Hide them until it's safe or convenient to move them or take them off the island to the mainland."

Viv groaned. "It's gruesome." She shook her head. "It's possible, I guess."

Lin's eyes widened. "Oh. Remember that feeling I got when I was at Mid-Island cemetery? I felt it twice. Maybe that feeling was trying to tell me that some graves have been tampered with there."

"Is it the same feeling as when a ghost is about to appear?" Viv asked.

"No. It's not the same sensation I get when ghosts are about to show themselves. When ghosts come, I feel chilly and the hairs on my arms stand up. When I'm near the bones, I get the feeling that someone is watching me. When I touched the bone, my fingers felt like electricity was zapping me." Lin remembered that she felt the zings on her fingers when she touched the metal locker where the skeleton was found. "And I get sort of dizzy. The feeling makes me think that someone is asking me for help."

Nicky was sitting up on the sofa, listening. He let out a small woof.

"I had that dizzy feeling at the cemetery when we were there. I felt like someone was watching me." Lin's voice was excited. "I wonder if someone has been tampering with graves there. Maybe that's why I'm getting those sensations." She stood up with an eager expression on her face. "Maybe some ghosts are trying to tell me they need help."

Viv frowned. "No. I am not going to that cemetery now." She folded her arms over her chest. "Absolutely not."

"You work all day. So do I. There are people around the cemetery during the day. This is the perfect time to go."

"No. This whole thing creeps me out." Viv got up and went into the kitchen. "What if the grave robber sees us? He might decide to kill us to keep us quiet."

Lin grinned. "You could bring the boning knife."

Viv ignored her cousin and busied herself making a cup of coffee.

Lin said in a sad voice. "I guess I'll just have to go by myself."

Viv whirled around. "Oh, for heaven's sake."

"I'm not trying to be a pain." Lin leaned against the kitchen counter. "Emily Coffin shows up whenever I'm close to the bones. She needs me to figure this out. The ghosts of those bones want me to help. I have to do it, Viv. It's an obligation."

Viv moaned. "I'm not letting you go alone. Just let me drink this coffee." She added milk and sugar to her mug. "Why can't our lives be normal? Why can't we just do normal things?" Viv took a gulp of her coffee.

Lin shrugged a shoulder. "Then I guess life would be boring."

***

Viv peered through the windshield from the passenger side of Lin's truck. Even though she knew the answer, she groaned, "Why does everything have to be done at night?"

Lin started to explain the reasons again, but Viv waved her hand in the air. "Oh, I know why it has to be done at night. My question was more of a lament. I'm whining about the situation."

The truck was parked in the small pull-out area near the entrance to the trail.

"Let's go." Lin, Viv, and the dog left the truck and started up the path through the woods. Lin flicked on the flashlight she'd brought along. After a few minutes of walking, Lin said, "It was right around here that I started to feel dizzy." She stopped and turned in a small circle.

"Anything?" Viv held her flashlight gripped in her hand like a weapon.

Lin nodded. "Yes." She took some steps off the path into the woods.

"Don't go any further." Viv looked over her shoulder to be sure no one was near them.

"I feel it again. Some dizziness, a feeling that I'm being watched." Lin came back onto the trail. "Let's keep going."

Nicky ran about with his nose close to the ground.

The wind seemed to be kicking up causing the leaves to rustle and tree branches to sway. The hoot of an owl could be heard off in the distance. The girls walked close together, their shoulders touching as they moved.

"I still feel it." Lin shut off her flashlight so as not to call attention to their presence should anyone be lurking around.

Viv glanced around the cemetery. "How do you want to do this?"

"I doubt anyone would be so bold to dig up a grave so close to the entrance to the cemetery or so close to the office. I think we should walk to the section that's more secluded." Lin pointed across to the small hill. "Let's hug the periphery so we can duck into the trees if we need to."

They walked slowly around the edge of the cemetery for about ten minutes. Viv said, "I didn't realize this was going to turn into a hike."

Lin grinned at her cousin. Viv wasn't eager for physical exertion so late in the day. They walked for a few more minutes and halted when they saw lights flickering between some trees.

Viv grabbed Lin's arm. "What's that?" she whispered.

Lin tugged on Viv's arm pulling her down into a squatting position. "Let's stay low so we can't be seen." She squinted trying to make out any movement up ahead in the woods. Nicky stood next to the girls, staring towards the lights.

"Is there a road over there?" Viv kept her voice soft. "Are the lights just headlights passing by?"

"There's a trail there. It's wide. I think it's used as a fire lane in case of a fire in the woods. It leads to a main road."

As they watched, the headlights went out.

Lin watched for movement. "There are a number of mausoleums over there. Someone could be robbing the crypts and carrying the bones to the car. Maybe they're doing it right now. Let's get closer."

Viv touched Lin's shoulder. "We're not going to confront them, are we?"

"No, if things look amiss we can call the police." Lin led the way to the tree line and they approached slowly and as quietly as they could.

"I don't see anything," Viv said. "I don't see anyone moving around near the mausoleums."

"I don't either." Lin stepped behind a large tree trunk and peered around it. "The car is still there though. Let's get closer to it."

Shielded by some trees, the girls stopped just a few yards from the vehicle. Someone was moving around inside. Viv gripped her cousin's arm as they tried to see what the person was doing. Suddenly

Viv let out a yip and slid to the ground. Lin wheeled and knelt to see what was wrong with her cousin.

Viv had her hand over her mouth.

"What's wrong?" Lin asked with concern, but then realized that Viv was giggling.

Viv gestured towards the car. "It's a couple. They're making out in the car." She couldn't hold in her laughter. Gales of giggles danced on the air and were so contagious that Lin started to laugh at the situation. Nicky joined in with several loud woofs.

The car's engine started up and the car screeched into reverse and hurtled away.

Between guffaws, Viv managed to say, "Guess we ruined their night."

CHAPTER 12

After Lin and Viv recovered from their laughing fit, they sat on the ground beneath the trees with Nicky resting on the grass in front of them. The night air was warm and pleasant and the cloud cover was breaking up allowing some light from the stars and moon to filter down between the branches.

"Those poor teenagers." Viv still had a huge smile on her face. "We must have frightened them."

The tension and worry of the past few days drained away as the girls chatted about things unrelated to bones and graves and unoccupied houses. The strong wind was dying down to just a gentle breeze that rustled the leaves overhead. The night sounds of insects calling to one another filled the air with chirps and clicks and buzzing.

Viv leaned back against the tree trunk and yawned. "What a beautiful evening. I could fall asleep sitting right here on the grass."

Lin took in a long relaxing breath and looked out over the dark cemetery.

"Shall we head home before I doze off?" Viv yawned again.

When the girls stood up, Lin shivered in the cool night air. She rubbed her hands over her arms to warm them.

Viv eyed her cousin. "Are you cold?"

"A little." Lin's eyes went wide and she slowly shifted her gaze from side to side.

"Do you see something?" Viv moved a step closer and took quick glances over her shoulders.

The dog whined and wagged his little tail. Lin followed the direction the dog was facing. Something shimmered by some gravestones and a form took shape. Emily Coffin stood transparent in her long dress with the high collar, her hair up in a loose bun. She raised her arm and pointed.

"You see something, don't you?" Viv whispered. She huddled close to Lin.

Lin gave a nod, keeping her eyes on Emily. The ghost remained with her arm outstretched for several seconds and then the shining particles of her form began to swirl, faster and faster until she disappeared.

"Is it Emily?" Viv's voice shook.

"She's gone." Lin looked in the direction that the ghost had pointed. "The mausoleums." She tugged on Viv's arm as she moved towards them. "We need to check them out."

Viv groaned, but followed Lin as she made her way towards one of the small stone buildings built partially into the hill. She flicked on the flashlight and moved the light up and down and from side to side over the stonework. "Everything looks intact." She adjusted the light so it shined on the lock. "It doesn't seem disturbed."

The girls moved to the next one and repeated the process while the dog hurried about with his nose to the ground. After checking all five mausoleums built into the hillside, Lin walked along a path that ran between graves and led to another small stone building. The girls inspected the outside stones and then went to the front to see if anyone had tampered with the door or the window. Lin pulled on the heavy lock attached to the door. It didn't budge.

"Maybe Emily was pointing to something else," Viv offered.

"She was definitely pointing to the mausoleums." Lin looked back at the group of crypts near the hill. "She pointed to those." Lin gestured back to where they had started. "Let's go back there."

"It's late, you know." Viv had her flashlight beam pointed at the ground. "We both have to get up early. Let's come back another time."

Lin had to agree that she was feeling fatigued and wouldn't mind crawling into her soft, comfy bed. She stopped and stretched. "Okay. We'll come back another time. I'm beat."

Viv clasped her hands together and looked

skyward. "Thank heavens."

Lin chuckled and slipped her arm through her cousin's. "Come on, Nick."

The dog wasn't with them. The girls stopped and turned to see the dog staring back at the road where the young couple had been parked earlier in the night. Lin called to him again, but he didn't budge.

"Now what?" Lin sighed and walked towards the dog. A few feet from the animal, she came to a dead stop. Coming from the dirt road, the sound of a car's engine floated on the air. It was getting closer. Lin scrambled back to her cousin, grabbed her arm, and pulled her across the grass to the tree line. "Get down."

The girls squatted.

"Nicky." Lin kept her voice down.

The dog dashed to Lin's side and sat next to the crouched young women.

"Is this spot lover's lane, or what?" Viv asked softly. "Is it just another couple arriving to make out?"

The girls stared through the branches and saw the car come to a stop where the dirt road met the cemetery boundary. The engine quit and someone stepped out. The person was wearing a hoodie. The face was hidden by the hood and the darkness. Reaching into the back seat, the person took something from the back seat.

"A duffel bag?" Viv whispered.

Lin raised her index finger to her lips to urge quiet.

The man headed down to the second stone building where he fiddled with the lock. The door opened and he disappeared into the mausoleum.

The girls exchanged wide-eyed looks. After about five minutes, the person reemerged, closed the heavy door, and carried the bag up the short hill to the car, where he got in, turned the vehicle around, and drove away.

"What was that all about?" Viv practically leapt to her feet. "What did he do? Who is he?" One hand was on her hip while the other hand flew about gesturing wildly.

Lin slowly rose from her crouched position. "It can't be anything above-board that he just did. It's nearly midnight." She let out a long sigh. "Did you notice what kind of car he was driving?"

"I couldn't see it very well in the dark. It just looked like a dark sedan. Maybe it was an older model? It seemed kind of big. Like a big old Lincoln?"

"I wish I had paid more attention to it." Lin started towards the mausoleum. "Let's go have a look."

When the girls and Nicky reached the front door of the tomb, Lin focused her flashlight on the lock. She moved it about and gave it a solid yank. The bolt unfastened. Lin blinked with surprise that the lock came undone. She leaned forward tilting her head so she could inspect the lock more closely. "This is clever work. Someone cut the bolt from behind. It looks fine until you see it from the back. It's cut so that it looks locked and it requires a good pull on it for it to loosen." Putting her hand on the large metal handle, she pulled the door open with a loud metallic creak.

"We're not going in, are we?" Viv fussed.

Lin stepped inside, shining her light along the crypts in the walls. Viv stayed in the doorway.

"There are five crypts. It's a family entombed here." Lin moved closer to see if any of the crypts looked to be tampered with.

Standing outside, Viv pointed her flashlight above the door. "It says 'Sparrow' above the doorway. That's the family name."

Lin moved her hand over the large marble squares in the wall that marked each crypt. A small central hole in a plate on the marble seemed to be a lock hole. She pointed the flashlight beam at the holes. "This is odd. There seems to be scratch marks on some of these crypts. I wonder if someone used a piece of metal to pick the locks." Lin tried to tug on the edges of the marble to see if it would move. "I can't open it."

"Oh!" Viv practically screeched. "Don't open anything. Lin, don't open those crypts."

"I wouldn't open it. I just want to see if it moves." Lin emerged from the mausoleum. "We need to report this. I'll call the police in the morning."

The girls and the dog followed the paths through the cemetery heading back to the trail that would lead to their parked truck.

"We need to come up with a reason why we were here so late at night." Viv kept nervously looking about the open space. "Or the police might think we're involved in stealing bones."

"Well," Lin tried to come up with an idea. "We could say that during the day we were biking on that dirt road that leads to the cemetery and you lost a necklace. We think you lost it when we were sitting in the cemetery resting before our return ride. We came back to look for it."

Viv narrowed her eyes. "In the middle of the night?"

"Maybe we could gloss over that part?"

"We better come up with something more believable than that," Viv suggested. "Why not just tell the truth?"

Lin tilted her head. "That I see ghosts and they want me to figure this out?"

Viv smiled. "No. Tell them you found those bones and you were reading on the internet about graves being robbed and wondered if this could be the case here. So we decided to come walk around and see if anything looked amiss."

"Won't they be suspicious because we're here late at night?"

"It's the only time we could both do it" Viv said.

"We have businesses to run during the day."

"Maybe." Lin thought it over and wondered how the police would handle the information. "I wonder if I should report it to Quinn first? Since he's the manager, he might want to be involved in the call to the police. I don't want to jeopardize our professional relationship."

"That's a good idea." Viv agreed. "Tell him in the morning and then you can make the call together."

The girls arrived at the entrance to the trail. "Where's Nick?"

Viv spotted the dog walking in the woods to their right. "He's there." She pointed. Out of the corner of her eye, Viv saw something and she hooked her arm through Lin's and pulled her behind the trees at the beginning of the trail.

"What?" Lin questioned her cousin's action.

Viv stared at the office building. "There was a light on in there, in one of the back rooms. Now it's out."

Lin turned slowly towards the cottage that housed the cemetery's office. "There aren't any cars parked over there. Could it have been a reflection on the window?"

Viv raised her eyebrows and made a face. "Isn't that what Quinn asked *you* when you told him you saw a light on in there? It was definitely a light."

The girls watched the building for ten minutes, but the cottage remained dark and they didn't see anyone leave the building.

"The person could have left from the side door." Lin sighed. "We should have split up so we could each watch an exit."

"What could someone be doing in there?" Viv frowned.

"Another piece of the puzzle." Tired and frustrated, Lin led the way down the trail to the truck and drove home to their waiting beds.

CHAPTER 13

Before meeting Leonard at the farmhouse site, Lin drove to the Mid-Island Cemetery to talk to Quinn. She and Nicky stood on the front stoop and knocked on the door. Quinn's car was parked in its usual spot so Lin was sure he was inside.

"Come in." Quinn called from the front room. "Oh, Lin. Everything okay? I wasn't expecting you today."

"I just wanted to talk to you for a minute." Lin and the dog went in.

"Sit down. Please." Quinn gestured to the earth-toned sofa on one side of the space. A coffee table stood on a rug of muted colors and a caramel-colored leather chair stood on each side of the sofa. A large desk was positioned near the windows with two chairs placed in front of it.

Quinn took one of the leather chairs. "What's on your mind? You're not quitting are you?" His eyebrows pinched together in an expression of worry.

"No, no, I'm not giving up the contract." Lin

smiled. She held her hands in her lap. "You've heard the news about the bones?"

Quinn nodded.

"I happened to be the lucky one who found the bones both times." Lin gave a weak smile.

"You? How did you happen to make both finds?" Quinn sat upright near the edge of the chair.

Lin explained about doing the landscaping at the farmhouse and accompanying John to the house showing. "My cousin and I were here last night. We saw something. I wanted to let you know about it before I reported it to the police."

Quinn's eyebrows shot up.

Lin spoke fast hoping if she spewed out information quickly, then Quinn wouldn't be able to poke holes in her explanation about why she happened to be at the cemetery late at night. "My cousin lost a watch at the end of the fire road on a bike ride. She works late. She owns the bookstore-café in town. I work late. We came last night because she realized she lost it and was upset about it and didn't want to wait until morning." Lin sucked in a breath. "We saw something ... near the mausoleums. A man got out of a car, and went into one of them. He looked to be carrying a duffle bag. When he left, Viv and I went to inspect. The lock on the door is cut in the back. That way, it doesn't look broken, but allows access by moving the bolt. In light of finding the bones, we wondered if they may have been taken from here."

Quinn had a look of alarm on his face. "Which mausoleum is it?"

"It says 'Sparrow' above the door. Shall I show you what I mean about the lock?"

Quinn gave a nod and stood up. He took a set of keys from the desk and when they left the office, he locked the door.

"When we were leaving last night, my cousin saw a light on in the back room," Lin told Quinn as they walked across the cemetery on the paths between the gravestones.

"There has to be some light reflecting off the window that makes it seem that lights are on inside," Quinn said. "You thought you saw lights there the other night. I wasn't here late last evening and no one else has a key. Nothing was disturbed in the office this morning. A reflection is the only explanation."

They walked up the incline to the mausoleums with Nicky following behind.

"It was that one." Lin pointed and they walked to the door. She lifted the lock up to show Quinn the cut on the back. Lin's eyes widened and her hand started to shake. "It was cut right here along the edge, but...."

Quinn leaned forward and craned his neck to get a look at the lock. "But, what?"

Lin rubbed the back of the metal with her fingers. Her heart pounded and a bit of sweat rolled down her back. She let go of it and it hit the door with a thunk. Lin's jaw tightened. "Somebody changed the lock."

Quinn stared at the young woman.

Lin's cheeks flushed and her breathing sped up. "It was cut last night. Somebody must have changed it. Maybe the person saw us here and changed the lock."

"Maybe it was a different vault? Let's check the others."

Lin didn't want to move from the spot. She knew this was the right mausoleum. Viv had read the name above the door. Grabbing the lock again, Lin yanked it like she had last night. She yanked on it again. It wouldn't budge. Fury rose in her throat. "We were here at this vault last night. The lock on one of the crypts looks like someone had been picking it."

Quinn looked at her, his mouth hanging open.

Lin's jaw muscles twitched. "Someone changed this lock."

"Did you and your cousin…?" Quinn hesitated. "Did you have a few drinks with dinner last night or maybe…?"

"We weren't drunk, Quinn." Lin folded her arms over her chest.

Quinn lifted his hands up in a helpless gesture. "Well, things seem fine now." Shrugging a shoulder, he said, "I'll have one of the caretakers check all of the mausoleum locks just to be sure they're functional." He nodded reassuringly. "Let's go back to the office. I'll talk to the caretaker right now."

Walking back to the front of the cemetery, Lin and Quinn remained silent. Lin knew he was questioning her judgment and she felt like a fool. Her mind was racing. The only answer was that someone saw her and Viv in the mausoleum last night and changed the lock. "I think I should tell the police what I saw last night."

"Oh?" Quinn said cautiously. "I'd really rather not have any bad publicity."

Lin shot him a look.

Quinn backtracked. "Well, if you feel like it's necessary."

When they reached the office cottage, Lin said, "Sorry for the confusion. I'll see you tomorrow." She hurried to her truck, let the dog in, and drove away.

Turning onto the street that would take her to the farmhouse, Lin drove along with her mind going a mile a minute. She pulled to the side of the road and reached for her phone to call Viv to let her know what had happened at the cemetery. Before she pushed the numbers, a thought popped into her head. She tossed her phone into her bag and started the truck, turning in the opposite direction from where she should be headed.

After driving a few miles, Lin took a left onto the fire road that led to the cemetery. She stopped the truck a few yards from where the car with the person carrying the duffel bag had been parked last night. She and Nicky got out and walked to the end of the road.

Lin saw the tire tracks of the making-out couple's car and then looked to the other side of the road. A smile crept over her face.

There was the second set of tire impressions in the dirt road right where the person's car had parked. Lin returned to the truck and took out her phone. She walked back to where the tire tracks were and photographed them.

We're not crazy, Quinn. We weren't drunk. And we aren't mistaken.

Lin walked to the end of the road and looked down the slight hill to the mausoleums. She stepped onto the grass and shuffled along keeping her eyes on the ground, moving them side to side. Reaching the Sparrow mausoleum, Lin kicked at the ground trying to find anything that might indicate that the lock had been changed.

She sighed. Leonard was waiting for her at the farmhouse. She had to give up her search.

Heading back to the truck, she was almost at the top of the hill when she saw something glint in the grass. At the same time she spotted the thing, Nicky found it in the grass and woofed. Lin rushed over, bent down, and picked up a curved piece of metal. It looked just like a section of a padlock shackle.

She winked at the dog and reached down to pat his head. "I think we found what we were looking for."

Sliding the piece of metal into her back pocket, a wide smile spread over Lin's face. *Someone changed that lock.*

CHAPTER 14

Lin jumped down from the small front loader and wiped her hands on her shorts. "It's looking great." She grinned at Leonard. "If I do say so myself."

"I agree, Coffin. Good work." Leonard was marking out where the new plant beds would go. The piles of dirt in the backyard of the farmhouse had been spread out and smoothed to prepare a nice level lawn area. Grass seed would be put down when the beds were edged, planted, and mulched. There was plenty of work to do, but with the mounds of dirt gone and spread, the yard appeared to be taking shape.

"The plants will be delivered tomorrow and Dave and Remy will be here to work with us." Leonard wiped his forehead with his arm. "Things should move pretty fast now."

The two joined the dog in the shade of a tree and Leonard placed his shovel on the ground. They both took long pulls from their water bottles. Leonard poured some water over his face and Nicky lazily raised his head to watch. The dog had been snoozing in the grass to avoid the afternoon heat.

Lin told Leonard about the cemetery adventure of the previous evening and her early morning visit to see Quinn at the cemetery. She explained about the person with the duffel bag who went inside one of the tombs, the lock on the mausoleum that had been cleverly cut, and the new lock that was on the door this morning.

Leonard rubbed his chin. "I don't like the idea of you and Viv sneaking around over there late at night."

"We weren't sneaking." Lin made a face. "Well, maybe we were."

Leonard gave her the eye. "If someone is up to no good, you could be putting yourselves at risk. It could be dangerous."

"We had our guard dog with us." Lin nodded at Nicky.

"He might not be enough." Leonard glanced at the dog. Nicky almost seemed to have a scowl on his face from hearing the man's words about him not being enough.

Lin pulled the elastic out of her hair and re-did her ponytail. "I wish we paid attention to that car. It was so dark, we couldn't make out much. The person was dressed in dark clothes, had on a hoodie. It was impossible to see what he looked like."

"Did you get the idea he was a young guy?"

Lin thought for a moment. "He didn't move like

an old man. His movements seemed kind of quick. He walked fast. He didn't seem stiff or anything. It seemed like he was in shape. Maybe young?"

Leonard's forehead creased in thought. "Did he hold the duffel bag different when he came out? Did it seem lighter going in or when the person was coming out? Could you tell by how he held it if there'd been a weight change in the bag?"

"Huh." Lin tried to recall the images of last night. She rubbed her temple. "I don't remember." She let out a groan. "I wish I had been more alert to the subtleties. Maybe Viv noticed."

A rustling in the bushes caused Lin and Leonard to turn towards the noise. Nicky gave a low woof. Olive from next door pushed through the foliage and emerged into the yard. "Hello!" she called. A plate of something covered with plastic wrap was in her hands.

The dog wagged its tail. Lin stood up from her sitting position under the tree and greeted the woman. She introduced Leonard.

"Things are taking shape, I see." Olive looked about the yard and then turned her eyes on Lin. "I heard on the news that a skeleton was found. I immediately thought of you since you were the one who found the bone here in the yard. Dreadful."

When reporting the finding of the skeleton, the news stories didn't mention the names of Lin and John so Olive was unaware that Lin had been the one who made the discovery. Lin didn't feel like sharing that fact with anyone. She didn't want people to start speculating that she was actually involved in hiding the bones.

Lin nodded. "It's very strange."

"What in the world does someone want with those bones?" Olive's voice was mixed with equal parts curiosity and indignation. "It's quite unnerving, isn't it?"

"It's a mystery, that's for sure," Lin agreed.

"Oh, I forgot." Olive pulled the plastic wrap back from part of the plate. "I made some brownies. Lloyd isn't one for sweets, but I love to bake and thought you might like some." She extended the plate to Lin and Leonard.

They each took a treat and thanked the woman.

"So what do you think is going on with those bones?" Olive's lips turned down as she looked from Lin to Leonard.

"Could just be kids up to nasty mischief. Summer vacation with not a lot to do can lead to trouble." Leonard devoured the brownie and Olive offered him another one which he gladly took.

"Kids? I didn't think of that. Well, they will be in loads of trouble if they get caught." Olive shook her head.

Lin didn't want to bring up her notion that the bones were being stolen in order to broker them for sale. "When I was here before, you mentioned that there had been a renter that you didn't like, the guy who rented the farmhouse in April and May a year ago. Do you recall his name?"

Olive stiffened. "That guy." Her shoulders seemed to shudder. "He gave me a bad feeling." Olive's upper lip curled. "Jonas Bradley. I hope I don't see him again."

"What did he look like?"

The woman's upper lip was still in its curled position. "He was average height, kind of stocky. Dark hair, cut very short, which didn't flatter him, let me tell you. He had a big, wide nose and deep-set eyes. I thought he looked like a serial killer." Olive blew out a sigh. "When I told Lloyd my impression, he said 'how would you know if he was a serial killer since you've never seen one before.'" She rolled her eyes. "I think people can tell things about others. You get a feeling, an intuition." She moved the plate she was holding around for emphasis. "So maybe he wasn't a serial killer, but he wasn't a good person, not at all. Nuh-uh. I didn't like him living next door."

"Do you know where he moved to?" Lin hoped Olive could answer her question.

"I don't know. Hopefully, far, far away."

"Do you know what he did for a living?"

"CPA. Certified Public Accountant. Some of his mail got delivered to our house by accident and that was printed after his name. Jonas Bradley, CPA. I wouldn't go to him to have any of my accounting work done, I'll tell you that."

Leonard removed another brownie from the

plate. Olive wrapped the remaining treats and handed the plate to Lin. "Here, you two enjoy the rest. Drop the plate off to me someday. I better get back. Lloyd will think I left him for someone else." She gave a shake of her head. "I don't know what that man would do without me." Olive waved and headed back through the bushes to her own house.

Lin looked at Leonard. "A serial killer."

Leonard guffawed. "I wonder what she tells her husband about us."

"She doesn't need to tell him anything about us." Lin took a sip of water. "I bet old Lloyd has plenty to say about us on his own."

"What are you thinking about this renter guy? Jonas Bradley. Are you thinking he has something to do with these bones?"

"Not necessarily, but remember I told you that Olive was sure Jonas was skulking around back here one night long after he moved out? It would be interesting to talk to him." Lin grinned. "Then I could see if I thought he was a serial killer."

"Well, you better not go talk to him alone." Leonard was only half-kidding.

"If I can find him, I'd just like to ask if he ever noticed any suspicious activity back here when he rented the place." Lin held her phone in her hand and moved her fingers over the screen. "I'm looking him up." She stared at the screen for a few seconds. "Look at this." A smile spread over her face. "What luck. Jonas Bradley has an office in town." Lin raised an eyebrow at Leonard. "I did have some questions about filing taxes since we just started a new business. I guess I'll make an appointment with Mr. Bradley." Her eyes twinkled.

Leonard picked up the shovel to return to work. "Well, go in the daylight. Don't meet him in the evening. Or take the dog with you for protection."

Nicky looked pleased by Leonard's comment.

"You want to come with me?" Lin asked Leonard. "Find out how to file our taxes considering we just started the business together?" Lin brushed some dirt from the seat of her jean shorts.

Leonard headed for the new flower bed he'd been working on. "I trust you'll tell me what to do." He paused, grinned, and added, "As usual."

CHAPTER 15

Walking down the brick sidewalk into town, Lin was so distracted by her thoughts that she turned her ankle on a loose brick and had to perform wild gyrations to keep her balance and prevent a crash to the ground. She muttered a curse under her breath. Wearing a red and white summer dress and a pair of sandals with a small heel, she realized that she had to be more careful strolling over the bricks. She'd been so used to spending her days in sneakers or work boots that she was feeling like a bit of a klutz in her new sandals.

A smile spread over her face thinking about sprawling onto the cobblestone street in front of Jeff when she went to meet him for lunch after her appointment in town. *Just call me grace, she'd tell him.* Lin couldn't wait to meet her boyfriend. She was looking forward to having some time away from bones and ghosts and trying to figure things out.

The reason for her mid-day meeting in town was two-fold. She wanted some tax advice since she'd recently started the landscaping business with Leonard, but talking to the accountant about the farmhouse and his time renting it was the first priority. Lin carried a leather folder containing a list of questions for the meeting and some blank paper to write notes.

Hurrying along one of the side streets in town, she looked for numbers on the front of the buildings and found the one she wanted. Inside, she climbed the stairs to the second floor office of Jonas Bradley, Accountant and Financial Advisor, and entered the small, but tastefully decorated waiting area. The receptionist's desk was empty. A wooden nameplate on the desk had "Chloe Waring" engraved in gold letters. There were signs that someone had been working at the desk so Lin looked around the space while waiting for the person to return. Diplomas and certificates attesting to Mr. Bradley's achievements lined the wall on one side of the room.

A tall, blonde, curvy woman in her twenties scurried in from the hallway and took her place at the desk. "May I help you?" she asked in an official tone, her posture straight and erect. The girl's long lashes framed her big blue eyes and the black and white dress accentuated the receptionist's figure.

Lin told Chloe who she was and that she had booked an appointment with Mr. Bradley.

"Mr. Bradley will see you." The blonde stood and escorted Lin down the hall to Jonas's office, opened the door with a flourish, and announced the client.

Lin had to bite her lip to keep from chuckling at the young woman's formal and forced behavior. It was like she was play-acting the role of a secretary-receptionist and her performance was way over the top.

Wearing what looked to be a very expensive business suit, Jonas Bradley stood and shook hands with Lin, his facial expression blank and emotionless. He gestured to the leather and chrome chair in front of his glass desk. Everything in the office was sleek and modern and Lin suspected that a decorator chose the things without input from the accountant who gave the impression that he might fit better with more traditional furnishings.

The man was exactly as Olive Sawyer described him. In his thirties, with deep-set eyes, a wide bridged nose, and dark hair, only it wasn't cut short any more. Lin wondered if someone had suggested that longer hair would better suit him.

Jonas Bradley was of average height, Lin estimated about five foot ten inches tall, and had broad shoulders which gave the sense that he worked out. There was something that Jonas gave off that made him seem uncomfortable in another person's company. Lin could see why Olive had felt uneasy with the man.

"So you're here for some tax advice." Jonas

asked some questions and made notes on a pad of paper. His questions were business-like and to the point. There was no chit chat or idle pleasantries to put his client at ease. The man was straightforward and had a brusque manner that suggested that he subscribed to the adage that time was money.

When questions were clarified and advice given, Lin attempted to make conversation. If she couldn't engage Jonas, then her most pressing purpose for coming to the office would be a failure.

Lin smiled. "I understand you rented a farmhouse out in Cisco for a while about a year ago."

The observation was so unexpected that Jonas's bushy, dark eyebrows shot up.

"The farmhouse has new owners. My partner and I have contracted to do the landscaping." Lin bumbled on not wanting Jonas to end the meeting. "I met the next door neighbor. She mentioned your name when I said I was in need of an accountant."

"You're the one who found the bone?" Jonas's eyes narrowed.

Lin swallowed. Her name hadn't been reported in any news stories, only that a landscaper made the discovery, so Jonas assumed that it must be her.

"Actually, my dog found it in the dirt."

"An unfortunate occurrence." Jonas looked like he might stand up so Lin quickly spoke.

"People are speculating about how the bone got there. A police search was conducted, but no other bones were found. I wonder how it happened to be on the property." Lin looked the man in the eyes.

"That *is* the question, isn't it?" Jonas's voice was steady and disinterested.

"It's very odd." Lin asked bluntly, "How do you think it got there?"

"That's for the authorities to determine." Jonas closed the folder in front of him. "Gossip and speculation are useless."

Lin groaned inwardly. "I suppose that's true." She nodded. "What was the backyard of the farmhouse like when you rented the home?"

Jonas stared at her. "Like?"

"You know, was there landscaping? Flowers?" Lin knew her questions were veering into nonsense, but she was desperate to keep the conversation going.

"I don't recall. I guess grass. I didn't spend any time in the yard."

"No? You didn't have to mow or do the outside upkeep as a renter?" Lin acted like she was fascinated with the man's experience living in a rental property. She knew he must think she was a nut.

Jonas frowned. "If *that* was expected, I would have found a different place to live."

"Who took care of the lawn then? Who did the mowing for you?" Lin questioned.

"A service came once a week."

Something flickered in Lin's mind. People from

a lawn service had access to the farmhouse's backyard. A worker could have hidden the bone there. "Do you recall what company it was?"

"I do not. The owner of the house made those arrangements. I had no interaction with the service."

Lin made a mental note to ask Olive if she knew the name of the landscaping company that took care of the yard when the farmhouse was being rented.

"May I ask why you moved out?" Lin smiled sweetly.

For a few seconds, the man looked like he wouldn't answer, but then he said, "It didn't suit my needs."

Lin wondered what that meant and what needs of Jonas's the house didn't meet. She decided that if she inquired about it then their meeting would probably come to an end so she kept the question to herself.

"You have a lot of questions about the farmhouse." Jonas's tone was almost accusatory.

A flash of annoyance shot through Lin's chest. She straightened in her seat, her expression serious. "I found a *human bone* in that yard. I held *someone's bone* in my hand. I think it only natural to have some curiosity and some questions about how it got there. Whose bone is it? Was foul play involved? Where are the rest of the person's bones?" Lin swallowed. "I think anyone who found a piece of a human being would wonder such things. Any compassionate person, anyway."

"Yes, well…." Jonas pushed some things around his desk top.

"While you were renting the farmhouse, did you ever see anything suspicious in the backyard? Someone trespassing? Anything that seemed odd?"

Jonas leveled his eyes at Lin and he blinked several times, his lids slow and heavy. "Why don't you ask the neighbor? Why don't you ask Lloyd Sawyer what he was doing in the yard one night?"

"Lloyd was in the yard?" Lin asked, and then remembered that Olive had told her that Lloyd went over to the farmhouse one night when he thought someone was prowling around back there. "Did Lloyd suspect someone was trespassing?"

"You'll have to ask him." Jonas checked his watch. He stood up. "I'm expecting another client now."

Lin got up from her chair. As she was walking to the door, she stopped and turned back. She wanted to see Jonas's reaction to her final question. "Olive mentioned that she thought she saw you one night behind the farmhouse. One night after you'd moved out."

"It may be that Olive has some trouble with her vision." Jonas's face hardened. "It had to be someone else, because it wasn't me. Perhaps her husband paid another visit to the rear yard after I moved out."

"Maybe so." Lin gave a quick nod and a forced smile. "Thank you for your time."

Lin showed herself out and hurried down the staircase to the first floor. Outside on the sidewalk, in the fresh air with people bustling around, she breathed a sigh of relief to be away from that man.

CHAPTER 16

"What did the police say when you reported what we saw at the cemetery?" Viv carried a plate with sliced mozzarella, crackers, olives, and cherry tomatoes to the deck.

"They wrote down my concerns and thanked me. That was it." Lin had stopped at the police station to talk to them about seeing the man enter the mausoleum and finding the broken lock which then had been replaced the next morning. She placed small plates for the appetizers onto the deck table.

"They weren't suspicious about why we were at the cemetery so late at night?"

"The officer didn't bring that up." Lin slipped napkins under the plates. "They must hear all kinds of nutty stories."

"You think the officer was doubtful about what we saw?"

"He probably wonders how in the world the lock could have been replaced so fast." Lin heard her front door open and Jeff call hello. "Which is what I wonder, too."

"At least you reported it." Viv scratched Queenie's cheek. The cat sat in one of Lin's deck chairs enjoying the sun. "Maybe the investigating officer will take it seriously."

Jeff came out to the deck carrying a bottle of homemade sangria and a six-pack of craft beer. He kissed Lin and greeted Viv, Nicky, and Queenie. Lin brought out glasses and they sampled the tasty sangria.

"Where's John?" Viv looked worried. As soon as the words were out of her mouth, John burst into the house and practically raced to the deck to join the others. He had a look of triumph on his face as he rushed to gather Viv in his arms and dance her around the deck. "I just closed on a deal," he announced as he twirled his sweetie around.

Sensing the happy mood, Nicky danced beside the couple and Viv giggled. She was happy and relieved to see John in such high spirits.

"It's a huge place out in Surfside." John beamed with joy. "Which means a huge commission for me."

Congratulations were given and the girls hugged him while Jeff shook John's hand.

"Too bad we don't have any champagne," Lin lamented.

"Homemade sangria will do the trick." John reached for the bottle and a glass. They all clinked their glasses together and settled into the cushioned deck chairs to chat and sample the appetizers. Lin had prepared a pasta salad with veggies and had chicken breasts baking in the oven. Viv had recently taken up bread making and she'd made fresh rolls which would be popped in the oven as soon as the chicken was roasted.

John told them all about the deal. "Now I'm thinking of getting a bigger boat." He grinned at Viv and waited for her to admonish him for being extravagant and not putting the money into savings.

His jaw dropped when Viv said and meant it, "Do whatever makes you happy." She smiled at John and hugged him. They all knew that Viv and John would marry one day, the couple just hadn't made it official yet. Viv and John had wanted to save money and grow their businesses before walking down the aisle.

"I wasn't expecting that." John chuckled, amazed at Viv for giving her blessing about a new boat. "It must be a trick of some kind."

Everyone laughed.

Conversation turned to island news and the new gig that Viv and John had secured to play once a week for the rest of the summer and into the fall. The manager of a downtown pub had caught a recent set that Viv and John's band played at a club and offered them a contract for the next eight weeks.

When Lin carried out the dinner and the four of them were enjoying the food, John brought up the bones. Viv glanced at him, surprised that he was the one who initiated the subject. She was pleased that his anxiety over finding the murdered young man in the empty house last month seemed to be coming under control.

Lin and Viv relayed their suspicions that a grave robber was at work and told about their cemetery adventure of the other night leaving out the part about Emily Coffin making an appearance.

John and Jeff stared at the girls with their mouths open.

"Grave robbing?" Jeff was appalled.

"It can be lucrative from what I've read." Lin passed the pasta salad to John. She told them the dollar figure that could be had for a skull and a full skeleton.

John was about to make a joke about quitting real estate to go into the bone market, but he was interrupted by Viv. "Please don't make a joke. It's just too awful."

"It's too bad you didn't get a good look at that guy at the cemetery." Jeff was still shaking his head. "Or at the car he was driving."

Lin told them about her visit to Jonas Bradley's office and her conversations with Olive and Lloyd Sawyer.

"It seems Jonas and Lloyd have something in common," John said. "They both have rotten personalities."

"And they both seem suspicious of each other."

The sun was almost fully set and shadows had fallen over the deck, so Lin lit the candles in the center of the table. "From Jonas's comments, it makes me think that he and Lloyd had a run-in of some kind, but Olive didn't allude to anything like that when she was going on about how she didn't like Jonas."

"It seems Olive would have said something if there was bad blood between her husband and Jonas," Jeff said.

"From what Lin tells us about Olive, I don't think the woman would hold back about a disagreement or whatever happened between Jonas and Lloyd." Viv reached for the platter of chicken breasts. "Olive seems pretty forthcoming."

"You know," John held up his glass of sangria and swirled the liquid around absent-mindedly. "I'm thinking about suspects."

"What are you thinking?" Viv's eyes met John's.

"I was giving the case some thought." John put his glass down and rested his arms on the table. "Who would have chosen the backyard of the farmhouse and the cellar of that house I was showing to hide bones? There are probably other places with bones hidden, too, but thinking about these two places specifically made me realize something."

"Tell us." Lin was eager to hear John's idea.

"The person would have to know that those two houses were unoccupied." John looked at everyone.

"A Realtor?" Lin's eyebrows shot up. "A Realtor is hiding the bones?" Her mind raced with the possibility.

"It doesn't have to be a Realtor," Jeff said. "But it has to be someone with access to that kind of information."

Viv leaned forward. "Someone who works for a lawn service would know that a house was empty."

"Someone who works at the post office would know, too." Lin added to the list.

"Or someone might hear about empty houses if he knows a Realtor or a service provider." Jeff leaned back in his chair. "The fact that a house is empty could come up in conversation. Someone hears about it and then uses the place to stash the bones."

John curled his lip. "I guess my idea isn't so great after all. There are a lot of people who have access to the information."

"It is a good idea." Lin nodded at John. "We can apply the idea to possible suspects. We'll need to consider how the suspect might know about unoccupied homes."

"Who are viable suspects so far?" Jeff asked.

"Jonas Bradley could be one," Viv suggested. "Olive thinks he's weird, Lin thinks he's weird. He had access to the farmhouse backyard."

"But did he know about the empty house on North Ave?" Lin wondered.

"He might have a friend with access to that information." Jeff opened a bottle of beer,

"Jonas doesn't strike me as someone who would have any friends." Lin made a face thinking about her interaction with the man.

"What about Lloyd?" Viv asked. "He seems odd from what Lin says and he was skulking around in the backyard. Why would he be over there? It's rude to be in someone else's yard, especially at night."

"And Jonas seems to suspect Lloyd of something," John noted.

Lin said, "The car we saw. At the cemetery. We should try to see what these men drive. Viv and I thought the car at the cemetery looked big, like an old Lincoln or something like that."

"It looked dark, too." Viv narrowed her eyes. "We need to spy on these guys and see what kind of car they're driving around in."

John thought of something. "What does Lloyd do for a living?"

Lin looked at John with a blank expression. "Why haven't I asked that question?"

"Let's see if we can find out." Viv got her phone out of her bag and tapped at the screen. "We'll look him up." After a minute, she said, "Here it is. He's a retired professor, writes books, lectures all over the world." Viv moved her face closer to the screen. "I bet he looks a lot better in this photo than he does in real life."

The Haunted Bones

Lin leaned close to Viv to look over her shoulder. "He does. Maybe that's an old photo taken when he was younger." She squinted to try to read the words on Viv's phone screen. "What does it say? What's he a professor of?"

Viv read aloud. "He's actually a medical doctor who also has a Ph.D. His area is forensic pathology."

"What does that mean exactly?" John asked.

Lin said, "It's figuring out the cause of death by examination of a corpse."

"Like a medical examiner," Jeff said. "Interesting."

Lin nodded. "Does his profile say anything else?"

"Oh." Viv's head snapped up. Her eyes were like saucers. "He's an expert in osteology."

Lin's jaw dropped.

"Osteology?" John looked puzzled.

Lin looked at him. "It's the study of bones."

CHAPTER 17

Lin carried several boxes of flowers to the side of the entrance of Mid-Island Cemetery. It was the first day she'd been back to work there since she'd talked to Quinn about seeing the person in the mausoleum and the broken lock on its door. She hoped Quinn was busy in his office and wouldn't come out to talk to her.

Nicky sniffed around the trees as Lin knelt and dug in the soil making small holes for each plant. The sound of a motor caused her to turn and see Quinn coming along the skinny road through the cemetery driving in an electric golf cart. He used the cart to get around the grounds more easily. Quinn waved to her and she groaned as he headed the cart in her direction.

"Morning." He stepped out and walked over to Lin

Lin stood and brushed the dirt from her hands. "Hi."

"I was going to call you this morning, but realized you'd be working here today so I waited to talk to you."

Feeling nervous and uncomfortable, Lin worried that Quinn might be about to fire her. She waited for him to continue talking.

"The police came by."

She sighed. "I had to report what my cousin and I saw. It wouldn't be right not to."

"I know, that's fine." Quinn gave a shrug. "It had to be done."

"What did the police say?" Lin wondered if the police did an inspection. "Did they check out the mausoleum?"

"Yeah. But I wanted to tell you that after you left the other day I talked to Tim, the head caretaker. He said he'd noticed that the lock on the Sparrow mausoleum was broken. It was discovered during a regular check of the monuments and vaults. When he went to replace it a few days later, the lock was fixed. He assumes that one of his crew changed it."

Lin stared at Quinn. She had been so sure that whoever drove up in that dark car the other night and went into the mausoleum had changed the lock, but it was a cemetery crew worker who'd done it. "So someone working here changed the lock?"

Quinn nodded. "Yeah. Who knows how long it was broken. There are regular checks on things, but you yourself said the problem with it was hard to notice."

"That doesn't change the fact that my cousin and I saw a man go into that mausoleum the other night."

"Tim checked the vaults. There didn't seem to be any issues."

Lin cocked her head. "What about the keyhole on the vault? It looked like something had been at work scraping the hole, like it had been picked."

"That kind of thing can come with time. Some of the marble can look scratched. It isn't indicative of anything wrong. It can be the natural aging of the stone."

"Did the police look inside the mausoleum?" Lin couldn't figure out what was picking at her about this development.

"I took them over there. Tim came with us. We went inside after we showed them the new lock. I told Tim what you'd seen. He was concerned so he opened the vaults to check the caskets. Everything was in order."

Lin narrowed her eyes. "Did he open the caskets?"

"Oh, no. We'd need permission to do that. Tim checked the caskets for tampering though. Everything was fine."

Lin looked across the cemetery to the hill on the far side near the mausoleums.

"The police think that maybe that guy you saw was using the mausoleum to store something. Drugs probably. They suspect the guy is a dealer and came to get his stash."

"That was convenient, wasn't it?" Lin had a

hand on her hip. "The guy cleaned out the mausoleum of the drugs on the very night we happened to see him."

"Maybe he noticed you and your cousin and decided to remove everything. Or it was coincidence." Quinn shrugged again. "The police suggested that we check the locks each morning for a while in case the guy comes back and wants to use the place for storage again."

Drugs. It was possible, Lin thought, but the whole thing seemed too neat. If someone was storing drugs in the mausoleum, it was a mighty big coincidence that he just happened to remove everything the very night Lin was present. She didn't buy it. "Well, I guess that's wrapped up then." Lin didn't want to share her misgivings with Quinn.

"I wanted to let you know." Quinn smiled. "You don't have to worry about grave robbers or anything like that."

Lin forced the corners of her mouth to go up. "Thanks. I better get these flowers in." She pointed. "I need to get to the next client."

"How's your truck running? Did you find out what was wrong with it?"

"I haven't had time to get it looked at. It took me five tries to get it going today." Lin picked up an eight-pack of white impatiens and started to plant them. "I'm going to have to replace it, I guess."

"I have a truck I want to sell, if you're interested.

It's used. Older, but it runs great. Let me know."

Lin thanked him and said she'd think about it. Quinn got back into the golf cart and headed away down the cemetery road.

As she planted and dug more small holes, Lin went over everything that Quinn had told her. She guessed the scenario he'd presented was possible. Tim, the caretaker said everything looked okay. He wouldn't have any reason to lie unless he was involved with removing the bones.

Lin had seen Tim around and had exchanged pleasantries with him. He was an older man who was the foreman of the place, assigning jobs to the younger guys that worked at the cemetery. Tim was definitely not the one she and Viv had seen with the duffle bag the other night. Tim had a crooked back and walked with a slight limp. The person they'd seen was easy and quick on his feet. It wasn't Tim.

It was certainly a coincidence that one of Tim's crew had changed the lock the morning after Lin discovered it was broken. She pushed off her knees and sat back on her heels, thinking for a minute. *The piece of metal that I found. The piece of the shank from the top of the lock. If that was part of the broken lock, why was it near the top of the hill by the fire road? If a guy from Tim's crew removed the broken lock, he wouldn't have carried it* up *the hill to the fire road.*

Nicky came up beside his owner and licked her cheek.

The Haunted Bones

Lin rubbed the wet spot and chuckled. "Nick, your kisses are awful sloppy." She hugged the little mutt and scratched him under his chin. Thinking about the piece of metal shank she'd found, she realized that it could easily be part of something else and nothing to do with the broken lock on the Sparrow Mausoleum. Lin shook her head. If she was going to figure out who was involved with these bones, she had to be more careful not to jump to conclusions. She sighed and went back to working on the planting.

Lin pondered how to make some progress on the case. She wanted to talk to Olive again to ask if she recalled the name of the company that had managed the lawn when the farmhouse was being rented. She also hoped to get Olive talking again about seeing her husband and Jonas in the backyard, and if possible, she wanted to talk to Lloyd. Lin and Viv needed to try to figure out if any of their suspects drove a large, maybe older, dark car.

Lin glanced over her shoulder. She hadn't seen Emily Coffin lately. She could sure use the ghost's help, but knew that the spirits only showed themselves when they wanted to.

She placed the last flower in the ground and pushed the soil around its roots. She watered all of the new flowers, and while winding up the hose, her phone dinged with an incoming text from Viv.

Can you get away? You need to see this. Meet

me around the corner from Jonas Bradley's office.

Lin sprinted to the truck with Nicky at her heels, praying that her vehicle would start.

CHAPTER 18

Miraculously, Lin found a parking space in town and she and the dog hurried along the streets dodging the tourists to Jonas Bradley's office building. She followed the side road that was the size of an alley that ran next to the building and led to a small parking lot tucked behind the offices. As Lin rushed down the road, she heard Viv call to her.

Her cousin stood across the street in an entryway to the back of a restaurant. Viv waved Lin over.

"What's going on?" Lin asked.

Nicky gave Viv a lick on her ankle.

"I had to make a stop at my dessert supplier." She gestured to the street Lin had turned off from. "I noticed Jonas Bradley's office sign when I left the supplier and I had to go to the bank so I took a short cut down this way. The parking lot is over there." Viv nodded towards the space. "I peeked at the cars as I went by." She paused for effect. "There's a large, dark sedan in there. It's in a space reserved for Bradley Accounting and Financial."

Lin's eyes widened and she turned to look at the lot.

Viv said, "We have to go over there to see it. I've been lurking on this side of the street in case Jonas came out. I only saw his picture on the internet and he's never seen me, but I still wanted to hide over here. I don't want him to see me."

"Let's go check it out." Lin and Viv and Nicky crossed the street and entered the lot which appeared to be only for owner or employee parking for the three-story building. The space was small, providing just ten parking spaces.

Viv pointed at the dark sedan, its front end facing the brick building. The car was an old, black Buick, but in very good condition. Lin bent to look at the tires.

"What are you doing?" Viv watched the door to the building. "Why are you looking at the tires?"

Lin stood up and fished her phone out of her back pocket. She slid her index finger across the screen and held it up to show Viv.

Viv squinted and lean close. "What's this?"

"It's a picture of tire marks in the dirt at the end of the fire road near the cemetery. I took the picture in case we could use it to match the tires on an actual car." Lin looked at the tire tread on the Buick and at the photograph. She sighed. "I don't know. It's hard to tell if it's similar."

Viv held the phone and took a turn trying to compare the tires with the ones in the photo. "Ugh.

How are we supposed to figure this out?"

Lin moved close to the side of the car and peered in through the windows to see if anything was on the seats.

"Don't lean against it," Viv warned. "There might be an alarm. That's all we'd need."

"There isn't anything on the seats." Lin straightened. "It's a coincidence, isn't it, that Jonas drives a car that looks like the one that was at the cemetery the other night?" She glanced up at the second floor windows. "I would love to question him with a lie detector test about where he was the other evening."

"He'd probably pass the test despite lying about everything. Come on, Lin, let's get out of here." Viv started away.

"Let me write down the license plate number, first." Lin reached into her small bag looking for a pencil and scrap of paper.

"Already done." Viv winked and smiled. She held up a piece of small note paper with the license number written on it.

The girls crossed the street and when they got to the other side, they heard the whomp of the brick building's back door slamming shut. They turned discreetly towards the lot to see if Jonas had come out.

Lin looked down at the sidewalk and let her hair fall around her face. "That's Chloe Waring. Remember I told you about her? The receptionist.

She works for Jonas. I don't want her to recognize me."

Chloe, with her straight blonde hair cascading down her back, held a key in her hand and moved briskly through the lot. She had on a tight red skirt, fitted white blouse, and black heels. A pair of dark sunglasses completed her outfit and made her look like a celebrity hurrying away from paparazzi.

Viv watched the young woman out of the corner of her eye. "Hey. She's getting into the Buick."

"She *is*?" Lin desperately wanted to look, but stopped herself.

"She's backing out." Viv flicked her eyes to the lot while she and Lin continued to walk slowly up the road. "She's turning in the other direction. There she goes."

"Is it *her* car?" Lin looked at her cousin with wide eyes.

Viv gave a shoulder shrug. "Or maybe she's doing an errand for Jonas and is borrowing his car."

"How can we find out if the car belongs to her?"

Viv said, "We could hide over here tomorrow morning and see who drives it into the lot."

Lin glanced back from where they'd come. "There isn't any place to hide though."

"We could park on the road and scrunch down. We might be able to see who drives up without them seeing us." Viv looked wary like she didn't want to actually do it.

Lin's face brightened. "Maybe we can find out where Jonas and Chloe live. We could maybe drive by their houses and see if that car is in one of their driveways."

"Figuring out where they live will be the trick though. We can check online later." Viv checked her watch. "I need to get back to the store."

"And I need to get to the farmhouse." Lin smiled. "Good thing Leonard is my partner, otherwise he might fire me." As they turned the corner, she took a quick look down the street. "We should have followed her."

"How?" Viv chuckled. "Run after her? She never would have noticed us chasing after her car."

***

Lin received a text from Leonard saying he was running late and wouldn't be at the farmhouse until later in the afternoon. She breathed a sigh of relief that her business partner wasn't already at the job tapping his foot waiting for her. Lin, Leonard, and the husband-wife landscaping team had completed a ton of work on the backyard project and Lin could easily handle the tasks of the day on her own. She replied to Leonard's text telling him she'd take care of the work at the farmhouse if he wanted to stay at the other client's property to get that work done. They agreed to meet bright and early the next day at the farmhouse to tackle the final parts of the project together.

Lin used the wheelbarrow to add loam to all of the planned landscaped beds. She hauled some of the plants to the beds and before putting them into the ground, she arranged them in their pots according to the plan. Stepping back, she checked the positions and the way everything looked together. Satisfied, Lin walked to the pile of tools that they kept near the house and picked up one of the shovels, but she changed her mind and placed it back on the grass.

She stretched and opened her cooler removing a cold bottle of water. The day was hot and Lin's tank top was drenched with sweat. Eyeing the patch of shade under the tree, she and Nicky walked over and sank down to cool off.

"I think it's the hottest day yet." Lin ran her hand over the dog's smooth fur while he lay on his belly watching the squirrels scurry about at the back of the property.

Lin glanced through the tree branches and bushes over to Olive and Lloyd's place. She couldn't see any cars in the driveway and wondered if either of them was at home. Lin decided to find out.

As soon as Lin knocked, Olive opened the front door and gave the young woman a broad smile. "Come in."

"I only have a minute and anyway, I'm a dirty mess. I'll stay out here on the porch."

Olive stepped out and closed the door behind her.

"I was wondering if you happened to recall the name of the landscaping service that took care of the mowing and trimming when the farmhouse was being rented."

Olive screwed up her face in thought and tapped the side of her cheek with her finger. She brightened. "It was a small company, just a man and his son. I don't know if they're in business anymore. I never see them around, at least not out this way."

Lin waited for Olive to tell her the name of the landscapers, but she didn't say anything. "What was their name?"

"Oh, of course." Olive tittered at her omission. "It was something like Thomas Mowing and Clean-up. Why do you ask?"

"Some of us were talking. We wondered if the lawn guys might have noticed anything odd going on at the farmhouse when they were working there." Lin left out the concern that one of the lawn guys might be the very person stealing the bones and hiding them. "I met Jonas Bradley the other day."

Olive's face looked like she'd sucked on a lemon. "Why?"

"An acquaintance suggested him to me to review tax issues for my new landscaping business. He has an office in town."

Olive groaned. "I hope I never run into him. What did you think of him?"

"He was very professional." Lin chose her words carefully. "He didn't have a lot of personality. No casual talk at all. Only business."

"That's about the nicest thing you can say about him." Olive glanced to the farmhouse. "I'm just glad he doesn't live next door anymore."

"Did he have a run-in with you or Lloyd?"

Olive was about to say something, but the front door opened and Lloyd's head poked out. "I wondered where you were. I heard voices." He looked at Lin.

"Hello," Lin said.

"We're just chatting." Olive's tone was slightly dismissive. Lin thought the woman probably picked up the tone from her husband and was now using it on him.

"Something I can help with?" Lloyd looked over his reading glasses.

"No, dear." Olive stared at her husband until he started to withdraw into the house like a turtle pulling back into his shell.

"What about lunch?" Lloyd asked.

"Soon, dear. I'll let you know."

Lloyd closed the door.

"You were about to say something about a run-in with Jonas?" Lin tried to jog Olive's memory.

"Was I? It was nothing." Olive bent and pulled a spent blossom from the huge container of flowers near the steps. "Would you like some lunch?"

Lin declined noting all the work she still had to do. She almost forgot to ask, but then the question popped into her head. "Do you remember what kind of car Jonas drove?"

Olive frowned. "He had a big old boat of a car. Black. In good shape, but really? Why would a younger man want to drive that ugly old thing? So old-fashioned. Lloyd liked the car. He loves all those big old things. Not me. Give me something fun or classy." She chuckled. "Or both." Olive checked to see if the soil in the flower pot was dry. "Right before Jonas moved out, he got a new car. A Toyota SUV. Not my style, but an improvement over what he'd had." Olive straightened. "Why do you ask?"

Lin lied. "Someone almost side-swiped me the other day. I thought the driver looked like Jonas. I wondered if he was unhappy with the meeting we had." She chuckled. "It was a truck that did it, so it wasn't him." Lin walked down the steps. "Thanks for your help."

"Anytime."

Lin heard the click of the Sawyer's front door shut as Olive went inside the house. A sensation of cold slid over Lin's skin and she glanced around to see if a ghost was nearby. Seeing nothing, she shrugged and thought her goose bumps must be from having been so sweaty and then standing in the shade of the porch while talking to Olive.

Walking into the warm sunshine, the hint of an idea flickered for a moment in Lin's brain, and then was gone.

CHAPTER 19

Lin, Jeff, Jeff's older sister, Dana and her husband, Andrew sat around the small pub table listening to Viv and John's band and sipping drinks. Lin agreed to go to the new venue on the condition that her cousin wouldn't call her up on stage to join them in a song. "I just want to sit with Jeff and relax tonight."

The place was packed and the band was getting a raucous reception. Lin had never heard her cousin sing and play so well. When the set was over, the band members walked through the crowd talking with friends and acquaintances while they took their break. Dana and Andrew headed for the bar.

Lin told Jeff the latest developments about Chloe Waring driving the dark car and about chatting with Olive Sawyer.

"Maybe Chloe bought Jonas's car when he got the new SUV." Jeff leaned on the table and watched the people milling about.

"So Jonas might not be involved with the bones at all." Lin held a glass of seltzer in her hand and brought it to her lips. "But what about Chloe?"

Jeff gave a shrug. "There are probably quite a few large dark cars driving around Nantucket. Just because Chloe drives one doesn't mean she has anything to do with the bones."

Lin pushed her hair back and groaned. "Nothing adds up. Nothing stands out."

"At least there haven't been any new bones showing up anywhere."

Lin sat up. Jeff's comment made her stomach feel icy cold. She scanned the room looking for ghosts. "Jonas and Olive seem to really dislike each other. Neither one says why though."

"Some neighbors don't get along." Jeff ordered a beer from the waitress. "There might not be any one thing that set off the dislike. Olive seems friendly and Jonas sounds the opposite. She may have found Jonas's behavior aloof and he might have found Olive intrusive."

"Why do you make so much sense?" A smile crept over Lin's lips and Jeff leaned down and kissed her.

Dana came back to the table. "No public smooching," she teased.

"Where's Andrew?" Lin asked.

"He's talking to someone he knows about buying a car." The noise level in the pub was increasing so Dana leaned forward to get closer to her brother and Lin. "He's just about run his car into the ground."

"How's your truck been running?" Jeff asked Lin.

She rolled her eyes. "I think I need to replace it. I need a reliable vehicle for my business. I just hate to spend the money."

"Maybe you should talk to Andrew's friend." Dana turned around to see if Andrew was heading back. "He sells used cars. We always buy from him."

"The manager of the cemetery where I have a contract told me he has a truck he's selling. I was planning to talk to him about it next time I'm working. If that doesn't work out then I'll try Andrew's friend."

"Quinn's selling a truck?" Jeff asked.

Lin nodded. "He told me it runs great."

Dana looked interested. "Is that Quinn from the Mid-Island Cemetery? He and his wife love cars. They collect them. He has a huge barn where he keeps them."

"How do you know Quinn?" Lin asked.

"I knew him in school. He was a few years younger." Dana smiled. "I should pretend I'm younger than he is. I run into Quinn and his wife from time to time. We have some mutual friends."

Lin said, "Recently he's had to go off island every week or so to take care of some family issues. I hope he's around later this week so I can make arrangements to see the truck."

"What family issues does he have?" Dana

increased her voice volume since the band was re-taking the stage.

"He said elderly problems. He didn't elaborate."

Dana made a face. "Really? His parents died right after he graduated high school. Maybe he means his wife's parents."

"Could be."

The music started up and some people hurried to a small dance floor to gyrate to the beat. Andrew had to maneuver around the patrons to make his way back to the table. He looked glum. Leaning close, he told them, "My car won't start. I was showing it to my friend as a trade-in and it not starting made a really good impression." Andrew gave a wry smile and looked at Jeff. "We'll need a ride home, if you don't mind."

"You want to go now?"

"We both have early mornings tomorrow," Dana told her brother.

Lin declined to go along for the ride to the other side of the island in favor of walking home and getting to bed since she and Leonard had arranged an early start time at the farmhouse.

It took some effort to get through the crowd, but Dana and Andrew shuffled along following Jeff who made a path through the teeming mass.

Lin sat for a few more minutes sipping her drink and enjoying her cousin's band until a few too many yawns convinced her to head home as well.

The Haunted Bones

***

The evening air felt refreshing after the crowded noisy pub and Lin sucked in a long deep breath. Walking along the brick sidewalks under the old-fashioned streetlamps, she looked in store windows and watched the people strolling past. Summer was her favorite time of year. Lin loved the hustle and bustle of tourist season, the sunshine, swimming in the ocean, and riding her bike along the many dedicated bicycle paths around the island.

Lin's thoughts turned to the bones and who might be responsible for hiding them. A wave of uneasiness engulfed her. She didn't feel that she was doing enough to find the culprit and she carried a heavy sense of responsibility about helping the spirits who showed themselves to her. There were a number of people who seemed suspicious or at least who could be possible suspects, but Lin didn't feel particularly drawn to any of them as the guilty party. Something was missing.

A couple passed her carrying ice cream cones and Lin suddenly had a craving for a sweet, cold, and creamy taste of ice cream. She turned into the pharmacy where a good-sized line of people waited at the small take-out counter to order their milky treats.

A little boy who was up way past his bedtime was fussing and clinging to his mother's leg. She bent and spoke kindly to him asking if he'd like to go home or would he like to wait and get the ice cream. If he wanted to wait, then he would have to be quiet. The boy rubbed his eyes with his little fist. He wanted the ice cream so he would stop fussing. His mom picked him up and he rested his head on her shoulder.

Lin smiled at the way the young mother had handled the crying and at the little boy who did what he had to do to get what he wanted.

A light went off in Lin's head. *Motive.* Who had motive to steal the bones? If she could figure that out, then she'd have a better chance to find the thief. Selling bones could bring in a lot of money.

Lin looked out the pharmacy window at the people strolling by. Just as she was about to move up in the line, something across the street caught her eye.

A tall, slender woman with long blonde hair hurried down the street. *Chloe?*

Lin left the ice cream line and stepped outside craning her neck to try to see the person. Catching a glimpse, she headed after the woman keeping her distance and trying to blend in with the crowd. After following for a few blocks, she was almost certain that it was Chloe Waring. Lin wondered if she lived in town and wanted to follow to see if she was heading home. Chloe walked towards the docks and stopped at the corner of the first boat slips. There were plenty of tourists strolling around the area, but Lin felt vulnerable and wanted to be sure she wasn't seen, so she stepped into a small shop and pretended to browse near the window display.

Chloe shifted from foot to foot and looked around like she was expecting someone. She wasn't standing directly under a streetlamp and Lin wouldn't have recognized her if she didn't have that long blonde hair which seemed to glow even in the meager light. Lin thought Chloe needed to push her white blonde hair up under a hat if she wanted to be discreet.

A man approached from the docks walking in a slow, relaxed way, but there was something about him that made Lin guess that he was meeting the pretty blonde. She watched as he walked up to Chloe, said a few words, and handed her what looked like a small white envelope. As soon as the exchange was over, Chloe moved an inch closer to the man, put her hand on his arm, and then turned around to head back up the street.

Lin squinted through the shop's window. The man watched the young woman for a few seconds as she walked away, then he headed back the way he'd come. As he turned to go, he stepped into the pool of light from the streetlamp. Lin's heartbeat sped up.

Quinn Whitaker from the cemetery.

CHAPTER 20

Lin sat at her desk in the small second bedroom trying to focus on the computer programming work she needed to get done for the company on the mainland. She really should be in bed, but she was so antsy after arriving home from seeing Quinn and Chloe together near the docks that she decided to try and focus on programming for a distraction. It wasn't working. Nicky was asleep on the rug at her feet and she looked down at him enviously.

After Chloe hurried away from Quinn, Lin tried to follow her, but got caught up in a crowd of tourists and lost sight of the young woman. Ever since she saw the two together, her mind had been working at the puzzle of what was going on.

She turned her desktop computer off and padded in her stocking feet to the kitchen where she put on some water for tea. Leaning against the counter, Lin wished she could talk to Viv about what she'd seen. It was too late to call so she'd just have to wait until morning. The tea kettle started to howl and Lin nearly jumped out of her skin. Taking a deep breath, she removed it from the burner and poured the water into the cup. A loud knocking on the front door startled her and caused hot water to spill over the counter. Nicky started to bark.

Lin whirled around with the kettle still in her hand. *Who could be knocking at this hour?* Her throat tightened and her heart raced. She walked softly to the door and peered through the peephole.

Leonard stood on her front steps.

Lin swung the door open. "What are you doing here?"

Nicky danced around the man to welcome him.

"Hello to you, too." Leonard looked slightly sheepish. "You okay?" He noticed Lin was holding a tea kettle. "You making tea or are you going to hit me with that?"

Lin stepped back to let him in. "You scared me to death when you knocked. If someone was about to break in I thought of pouring boiling water over him."

Leonard's mouth turned up in a grin. "Good thinking."

The two walked to the kitchen with the dog still wiggling around Leonard.

"It's kind of late for a social call." Lin took out another mug. "Tea?"

Leonard nodded. "I was out. I was driving home and I...."

Lin turned slowly around and cocked her head. "And what?"

Leonard shifted around uncomfortably. "I saw you had the lights on so I stopped."

Lin didn't believe a word of it and said so. "What's the real reason you're here?"

The creases in the man's face seemed to deepen and worry lines showed at the corners of his eyes. "I just wanted to make sure you were okay."

Lin put a hand on her hip. "Viv could have been staying over or Jeff might have been here. You know those things. Why wouldn't I be okay?" Lin thought back to the last case she'd looked into. The murderer ended up sitting in her living room and when he attempted to attack her, Leonard happened to show up at that very moment.

A shiver ran down Lin's back. She leveled her eyes at the man. "Did you have some sense that I wasn't okay?"

"What?" Leonard sputtered. "No."

"Because if you did, then tell me." Lin glanced at the kitchen door that led to the deck. She hurried over and locked it. She tried to remember if she'd locked the front door when she'd let Leonard in. "Leonard, did you or didn't you sense something?"

He looked down at the floor. "Maybe."

Lin rushed to the front door and bolted it. She hurried about the room turning off the lamps so somebody standing outside couldn't see into the room. When she returned to the kitchen, her eyes were wide and her hands were shaking. Leonard wouldn't make eye contact with her.

Lin touched his arm. "You need to be straight with me. What did you feel?"

Leonard turned around and poured himself a cup of tea. "It's just stupid. I shouldn't have come."

Nicky sat at the man's feet and whined.

"Take it seriously." Lin hesitated and then said, "I get feelings, too."

The big man slowly moved to face Lin. He seemed to be wrestling with something. "Okay. I wasn't out, I was home watching TV. I felt all cold inside and I had a feeling that you weren't safe. It was a strong feeling. I had to come over. When I got here, I saw the lights were on and no one's car was out front, so I knocked. Now you probably want to have me locked up."

Lin smiled. "Thank you. For coming over even though it seemed silly." She teased him. "You could have just called."

"Somehow, that didn't seem effective enough at the time." Leonard took a swallow of the tea. His cheeks were flushed with embarrassment. "I guess I can go now."

Lin sat down on one of the stools at the kitchen island. "Stay and finish your tea. I need to talk to you."

***

Lin told Leonard everything that had happened since she and Nicky found the bone behind the farmhouse even though he'd heard some of it before. She did leave out the part about seeing ghosts.

"Jeff's sister is right. Quinn's parents died years ago. So he isn't taking trips to the mainland to help out his elderly parents. Quinn's wife, Brin, her parents are dead, too, so he isn't going to the mainland to help his in-laws either."

Lin looked at Leonard with a smile. "Quinn and Brin?"

"I know, huh?" Leonard rolled his eyes. "They're like characters in a kid's story."

"What could Quinn be doing with Chloe Waring?"

Leonard shrugged. "Affair?"

"I wonder what he handed her in that envelope tonight." Lin put her chin in her hand. "Could they be working together? Stealing the bones together? Selling them? Maybe the envelope had her cut of the money in it."

"Quinn works at the cemetery." Leonard thought things over. "That would make it easier to steal bones. But why is the girl involved? They're having an affair and they hatched a plan to steal and sell bones? Seems pretty weird."

"I've been trying to come up with a motive. All I can think of is money. Human bones and full skeletons bring in a hefty sum. I looked it up. Money seems like the only reason to do such a horrible thing."

Leonard shrugged. "Money is a powerful motivator."

"Could Quinn be in some financial trouble? Maybe he needs money and happened to read about grave robberies and decided that was the answer to his worries."

"I've lived on Nantucket for almost forty years. I know a lot of people, but I don't know their personal issues. Well, some I do, but I haven't heard anything about Quinn."

Lin sighed. "And then there's Jonas. Olive Sawyer thinks he's trouble. He used to drive that old dark sedan. Maybe he still does. Maybe Chloe was just borrowing his car when Viv and I saw her driving it."

"And then there's Lloyd." Leonard took a can of seltzer from the fridge and popped it open. "What did you say he was an expert in? Some kind of bone thing?"

"Forensics. Osteology. The study of bones." Lin rubbed her temple. "I'm getting a headache from all this. How will the bone thief ever be caught?" Her voice carried a tone of despair.

"Maybe the person will make a mistake." Leonard sipped from his can.

The sound of shattering glass and a loud crash in the front room shook the house causing Lin to let out a shriek and the dog to start howling. Leonard was on his feet in a flash and dashed for the living room. Lin and Nicky were right behind him.

They all stopped short at the threshold to the living room when they saw what had rolled across the floor after being thrown through the window. Lin gasped and turned away while Leonard stepped closer. Nicky approached and sniffed.

A skull rested on the floor, its eye holes gaping up at them.

Leonard knelt down. "It's not real. It's heavy plastic. A brick came through the window first then this must have been lobbed in after it." He picked it up.

Lin breathed a sigh of relief that the skull wasn't real, then almost immediately her relief was replaced with rage and she started to rant. "Who would do this? What a terrible thing to do."

Leonard ignored the rant. "There's a note inside." He removed the pale blue rectangular piece of paper and unfolded it.

Stay out of it

"You want to call the police or should I?" Leonard asked.

"You know how you said maybe the bone thief will make a mistake?" Lin turned her eyes away from the paper to look at Leonard. "I think they just did."

CHAPTER 21

Lin had seen the blue pad of paper on Chloe's desk when she was there for her appointment with Jonas. "So the note that came through my window last night with the brick could have been written by Chloe." She fiddled with her horseshoe necklace as she finished telling Viv about the events of the last evening. The café was buzzing with early morning customers' conversations. People stood in line to order, sat at the tables and on the comfy sofas, and stood talking in small clusters holding coffee and tea cups and nibbling on bakery treats.

Viv's lips pressed into a tight thin line and she wiped her hand on her blue apron. "Chloe might have seen you tailing her or maybe she saw us at the parking lot the other day when she drove away in the dark car."

"If she's working with Quinn then she knows my suspicions about the mausoleum and the lock and that someone is up to something at the cemetery. Quinn would have told her."

"I'm so glad that Leonard was with you last

night." Viv greeted a regular customer with a smile and a nod and then gave her cousin a worried look. "I'm glad you weren't alone in the house." She shuddered. "God. A brick through your window."

"Don't forget about the fake skull that came along with it." Lin glowered. "Where do you even get such a thing?" Finishing the last of her latte, she handed the empty cup to Viv. "You know, that's the second time Leonard has shown up when I've been in trouble." Lin narrowed her eyes and leaned against the serving counter. "He must have really good intuition or he has some powers that he doesn't seem to be aware of. He's uncomfortable about it, brushes it off as silly nonsense."

John swooped around the corner wearing a tan summer-weight suit and a starched white shirt and approached the counter for his usual black coffee to go. "I've got some gossip." His eyes twinkled as both girls moved closer to him.

"My friend at the police station told me that some officers asked to be let into the mausoleum that had the broken lock. They wanted all the crypts inside opened to check that none of the bones had been stolen."

"And?" Lin was eager to hear what they'd found.

"All the bones were present and accounted for." John picked up the take-out cup.

"Huh." Lin looked across the room. "Why was that person we saw wearing the hoodie inside the mausoleum then?"

"Maybe he heard or saw us and got frightened away." Viv wiped the counter with a cloth. "We spoiled his plans, I bet."

Lin asked John, "Did the police order any of the other mausoleum crypts to be checked?"

"My friend only heard about the one you'd complained about." John leaned over the counter and gave Viv a quick kiss and then was off.

"John seems a lot less nervous about showing unoccupied houses." Lin watched the young Realtor hurry away to see a client.

"I'd been nagging him to talk to a therapist about finding the murdered body in that house. At first, he was very against it, but right after you found the skeleton at the house he was showing, he decided it might be a good idea to make an appointment with someone to talk about his anxieties. He's seen the therapist three times and already he seems less worried. I think it's been good for him."

Lin put some money on the counter to pay for her drink. "I'm proud of him. It can be hard to ask for help."

"That is a foreign concept to me." Viv chuckled. "I have no problem asking for help of any kind."

"Speaking of needing help...." Lin eyed her cousin.

Viv's face lost its smile and she took a step back. "I said I have no trouble *asking* for help. Giving it is another story."

Lin ignored the statement. "We need to find

evidence that Quinn and Chloe are stealing the bones."

Viv crossed her arms over her chest. "I'm listening," she said warily.

Lin lowered her voice to a whisper. "We need to look in the cemetery office. See what's in there. Files. Records. We need to look around and see if there's anything that can link the bones to Quinn."

"The office." Viv's blue eyes flashed. "At night, I assume."

Lin nodded.

"How will we get in there?"

One of Lin's shoulders shrugged.

Viv's eyes went wide. "Break in?"

"Shh." Lin held her finger to her lips. "Not exactly break-in."

"I am not doing anything illegal." Viv had her hand on her hip.

"We won't. Well, you won't. If we get caught, we'll just say we knocked on the door and it happened to open. Someone mustn't have pulled it tight when they left." Lin raised her hand in a helpless gesture. "It happens."

"How would we really get in? You don't know how to pick a lock."

A broad smile spread over Lin's face. "Yet."

***

"Jiggle it a little." Leonard mimicked how to

move the thick piece of wire.

Lin knelt on the porch in front of the door to her house. She'd already mastered opening the lock on her back door and the ones at Leonard's house. This one was proving difficult.

Leonard held his hand in the air and mimed how to move the pick. Lin watched and gave it another try. *Click*. The door opened. Lin beamed at the man standing next to her and let out a whoop at her success. "I knew you'd be able to help me with this."

Leonard looked serious. "Of course, I don't condone this sort of behavior. I'm just teaching you a new skill. In case you get locked out of your house someday."

"Thank you." Lin smiled and put the pick in her back pocket. "I'm sure it will come in handy." She winked. "How'd you learn to do it?"

They sat down on the front steps. "I was in the military."

Lin laughed. "That's what they teach you in the military? Jeff was in the Air Force. I'll have to ask him if this was one of the required tasks he had to learn."

Leonard stood up. "Are you still going out to Quinn's house to look at that truck?"

"Yeah. Tomorrow. I thought it might be helpful to go to Quinn's place to see it. Maybe I can find something that links him to the bones. I told him I was going to be out that way anyway, so I'd swing by." Nicky sat on the porch and rested with his side pushing against his owner. His eyelids started to close.

"Take Jeff with you," Leonard said. "Don't go there alone."

"I'll have my trusty dog with me." Lin nodded at the little brown dog.

"You might want a little more power in your protector." Leonard headed to his pickup. "Ask Jeff. If he can't go, then call me."

Lin waved to Leonard as he pulled out of the driveway and on the way inside she glanced at the piece of plywood that Jeff had hammered over the broken window. A sigh slipped from her mouth. She had to have some proof before she told the police who she suspected of stealing the bones.

Lin fed the dog, warmed some leftovers and ate her dinner while she did programming work at the desk in the spare bedroom. Halfway through her tasks, she turned away from the computer screen and looked out the window to the dark side yard. Thinking of the sound of last night's shattering glass, Lin's throat tightened.

Feeling like she was being watched, she went to the window and pulled down the shade to help her feel less exposed to the outside. Her body buzzed like she'd had too much caffeine. Sitting back at her computer, Lin tried to pick up her work where she'd left off, but it was no use. Unable to focus, she logged out and turned off the screen.

The Haunted Bones

Walking into the kitchen for a cup of tea, Lin thought she caught a glimpse of movement on the deck. She froze while taking a mug from the cabinet. Afraid of what she might see, she stood in place facing the cabinet, but trying to see out of the corner of her eye to the deck. Lin's posture shrank as she braced herself for an object to come flying through the glass.

A sudden wave of cold engulfed her and she sucked in a breath. She looked to the deck.

A man stood next to the deck table, unmoving, staring at Lin. His transparent body shimmered. He seemed to be in his late twenties and wore a brown three-piece suit, at least it looked brown in the feeble light of the old security lamp that shined onto the deck from the roof. The style of the suit and the cut of the man's hair gave Lin the impression that the garment and the haircut were from the 1940s. The man's facial expression was emotionless. Lin noticed that one of the ghost's legs was missing below the knee.

She closed her eyes and tried to clear her mind hoping that she might receive a mental message from this new ghost. Lin breathed in and out in a slow easy pattern. Several minutes passed and Lin started to feel less cold. Her eyes flew open, afraid the ghost was about to leave.

Suddenly, the spirit's arm rose in the air and extended, the finger on one hand pointing up to the roof over Lin's bedroom. His eyes locked onto hers and then the atoms of his body glimmered and swirled and he was gone. Lin's eyes followed to where the man had pointed.

Three little birds sat on the gutter at the edge of the roof. Sparrows.

Sparrow. That was the family name of the mausoleum that had the broken lock at the Mid-Island Cemetery.

CHAPTER 22

Lin, Viv, and Nicky walked along the trail that led from the small parking spot to the cemetery. It was a clear night with the stars shining and a slip of the moon showing bright against the midnight sky.

"That's all the ghost did?" Viv asked. "He just pointed to the sparrows and disappeared?"

Lin carried a small backpack over her shoulder. "The Sparrow mausoleum is a clue. That's what he was telling me." The girls walked slowly trying not to step on any sticks that might snap and give them away. Lin kept her voice soft. "The ghost was missing part of his leg." She reached down and pointed to her calf. "I bet the leg bone that Nicky and I found belongs to last night's ghost and I bet he's a member of the Sparrow family and is buried in that mausoleum."

A sharp breath escaped from Viv's throat. "Oh." She gripped Lin's arm and kept looking over her shoulder.

"It's okay, Viv." Lin chuckled at her cousin's concern about ghosts. It wasn't ghosts they had to be worried about. "Anyway you can't see ghosts so you don't have to be afraid that Mr. Sparrow will appear here."

"You don't see him do you?" Viv's voice was breathless with worry.

"You're the only one I see." Lin smiled. "For now."

The girls approached the cottage that housed the cemetery office. No lights could be seen inside and no cars were parked nearby. "Let's go up and knock on the door in case someone's in there." Lin led the way up the steps and rapped her knuckles against the door. "Here's a bell." As she put her face up to the window in the door, she pressed the small button and heard the chimes ring inside. "It's all dark. No one's here."

Lin put the backpack on the landing and rummaged through it. She handed Viv the flashlight and took out the wire pick she'd been practicing with yesterday. "Where's Nicky?"

Viv gestured to the wooded area behind the cottage. "He's back there. I can hear him rustling around in the bushes." She flicked the flashlight on and held the beam to the doorknob. "I hope there isn't an alarm."

Kneeling on her left knee and raising her hand to the lock on the knob, Lin looked up at her cousin. "I hadn't thought of that." Turning back to work the lock, she said, "If it goes off, run."

"You don't need to tell me twice." While Lin

The Haunted Bones

worked with the pick, Viv kept swiveling around to look behind her.

"Viv." Lin couldn't see because Viv had shifted the light too far to the right while she'd been searching over her shoulder.

"Sorry." Viv adjusted the beam.

After ten minutes of fiddling with the lock, Lin let out a groan. "I can't get it. Let's go to the back door." The girls moved to the rear of the cottage and Lin started in on the lock with her pick. While Lin was cursing the lock, Viv noticed the large window box of petunias that was perched next to her on the railing of the small porch. She saw a small rock in the left corner of the box. Lifting it up, Viv smiled as she removed a small object from its hiding place.

"Why don't you try this?" Viv handed it to Lin.

"A key?" Lin rolled her eyes. "Where did you get it?"

Viv pointed and Lin shook her head, stood, and opened the back door with the key. "I guess whoever was in here those two nights we saw lights on in the back room found the key, too." She pushed the door open. "We shouldn't turn on the lights. We'll have to use the flashlights, but let's be careful to keep the beams low." She reached into the backpack and retrieved another flashlight. "Let's leave the door ajar while we're inside in case Nicky wants to come in."

They moved to the front room and walked about

the office and Quinn's desk. Viv opened the drawers and moved some papers around. Lin walked softly to the credenza and slid the doors back to see what was stored there. "Nothing interesting. I'm going to the back room. That's where we've seen lights on. Let's check it out."

File cabinets lined three walls of the room and there was a long table placed in the center. Lin walked to the furthest cabinet on the left. She bent down and lifted her flashlight. "They seem to be arranged by name."

Viv inspected the files on the opposite side of the space. "These have dates on the front."

Lin sighed. "How are they filing things? Are they cross-filing everything?" She pulled open the top drawer and checked the files. "These records are filed by date and then there are folders with names within the larger date file."

"I'll start going through these." Viv removed some files and opened them. "It might take us a while to find anything useful."

Twenty minutes passed. Lin straightened up. "Was there a date engraved anywhere on the Sparrow mausoleum?"

"There was a year on the stone." Viv tried to picture the front of the building. "I know it was late eighteen-hundreds. Maybe eighteen-eighty something?"

Lin moved the beam of light across the fronts of the cabinets. "Here." She pulled out a file.

"Sparrow." Her voice held a note of triumph. Placing the folder on the table, she poured over the information. "There seems to be five people buried in that building. The last one was Michael Sparrow, born 1922 and died in 1945." She looked up at Viv. "It's my ghost from last night. Maybe he died in the war." Lin returned her attention to the file. "That's all the information."

"What did the ghost want you to find? Just his name?" Viv came over to stand next to her cousin.

Lin's heart started to pound. "When the police came to check that the bodies weren't disturbed in the Sparrow mausoleum, I wonder if they just checked to see if there was a skeleton inside. I bet they didn't check to see if all the body parts were there."

"Michael Sparrow's leg bone," Viv said. "They saw a body was in there, but they didn't notice the leg bone was gone."

"I need to talk to the caretaker. He was at the inspection. I'll ask him about it. Why was that tomb targeted?" Lin pushed her hair back and started looking through the file again. When she turned her head to look at the other cabinets, a whoosh of dizziness washed over her and she grabbed the table to keep her balance.

Viv noticed and took hold of Lin's arm. "What is it? Is there a ghost?"

Lin slowly straightened. "It's old. That's the reason. The Sparrow mausoleum is old. There probably aren't any relatives left alive." Lin's voice shivered with excitement. "No one would notice if the mausoleum was tampered with. The thief must be stealing bones from tombs that are old, that way there's no one to notice any signs of a break-in."

"We should check the locks on some of the older mausoleums." Viv made sure that all of the files she looked through were put back properly.

When things had been straightened up, the girls left the cottage. Nicky was sitting on the grass at the bottom of the steps and he stood up and wagged when he saw Viv and Lin. As Lin was locking the door, a wave of nervousness or anxiety came over her. She paused trying to figure out what was causing the sensation.

"Come on, Lin. Let's get out of here." Viv and Nicky started off towards the far end of the cemetery.

Lin shook herself, turned the doorknob to be sure it had locked, and hurried after her cousin. They walked along the path to the older stone tombs where Viv pointed the light around looking for dates carved into the entrances. Lin used her light to inspect each lock from the front and back and she yanked on them to see if they might come loose. Everything appeared to be in order.

Viv yawned. "Let's go home. It's so late."

"There are only two left. We may as well finish." Lin practically had to drag her feet up the slight hill to the last buildings. She wished she was at home in her bed covered over with a soft blanket. Impatience and annoyance that she wasn't making enough progress with this case picked at her and made her feel weak and out of sorts.

The girls repeated their routine and again found nothing.

Viv said, "It's just like the last time we checked the locks. Nothing seems to be wrong with any of them."

As they trudged to the next mausoleum, little sparks twinkled in Lin's vision and she groaned thinking that a migraine was coming on. She pushed her finger against her temple and rubbed. Her backpack slipped off her shoulder and thumped to the ground.

"This one's really old." Viv was looking up at the beam of light encircling the date stone. "Did we miss this one last time we were here?"

Lifting up her backpack, Lin shifted her eyes to the final mausoleum and had to snap her eyes shut from the blinding light emanating from between the building's stones. She shielded her eyes and turned her head away.

"What's wrong with you?" Viv took a step closer and stared at her cousin.

Lin blinked. The light was gone. She told Viv what had happened. Lin's heart pounded and she felt light-headed. "What's the name on the building?"

"Stacey."

Pings of recognition bounced in her head, but she couldn't figure out why. Lin walked to the front of the structure. Long vines grew over the roof and both sides of the mausoleum which, like the others, was partially tucked into the hillside.

Nicky let out a deep bark that made both girls jump.

"Shh," Lin told the dog. "No barking, Nick."

A wrought-iron gate was built in place to swing over the front door. The heavy old lock on the gate did its job and wouldn't budge when Lin gave it a yank. There were no indications of it being cut or tampered with in any way.

Viv let out a long sigh followed by an even longer yawn. "This is a goose chase. Let's go home."

Lin's shoulders drooped with disappointment as she tried to reconcile seeing the light shining out of the stones with finding the mausoleum locked up tight. Shaking her head, she noticed something near the bottom of the gate. She ran her hand down one of the gate's iron posts to the bottom and her eyes widened. Lin followed the post up to where the top hinge attached to the building. "Viv." The word floated on the air.

Viv stopped.

"This gate."

Viv hurried over and pointed her flashlight where Lin indicated.

"This part has been removed." Lin indicated a

section of the gate. "This part of the gate isn't attached to either side." Lin's heart nearly exploded with excitement. "Help me. Push here."

A section of the gate slid back just enough to give access to the heavy door to the tomb.

"Well, well." Viv put her hand on her hip. "Someone thought they were pretty clever rigging the gate like that."

Lin could feel that the back of the lock on the door to the mausoleum had been cut. She yanked on it and the shank released. "They thought their sneaky manipulation of the gate would let them get away with breaking in here."

"They *did* get away with it." Viv cocked her head and smiled. "Until now."

CHAPTER 23

Lin knocked on the door of Nantucket historian Anton Wilson's home. The door swung open a second after Lin lifted her hand from it.

"Carolin. Right on time. Come in." Anton led Lin and Nicky into the country kitchen at the rear of the antique house. The dog curled on the rug in front of the fireplace and Lin and Anton sat at the old worn wooden table.

Anton was thin and wiry and had gray hair combed back over his head. He wore black frame glasses that often slid down his nose requiring that he give them a push back into place. Anton's manner could be intense and Lin was slightly afraid of him when they'd first met.

A tray was set in the center of the table with a carafe of coffee, a jug of iced tea, a creamer and a silver bowl of sugar cubes. Coffee cups and tall glasses stood at the ready beside a plate of assorted cookies.

"Help yourself." Anton had diagrams and family trees and books and papers spread all over the table top. He loved island history, had written many books on the subject, and would spend hours discussing it with anyone who showed the slightest interest.

Lin poured a glass of iced tea for each of them. She passed the sugar bowl to Anton and took a ginger cookie from the plate.

Anton started to lecture about the Coffin family who were early settlers of Nantucket and pointed to the different branches of the family on the huge sheet of paper that was only one small part of the generational line. Lin munched her cookie and listened as Anton rattled on becoming more excited and animated as he went.

After fifteen minutes, Lin sipped her drink and cleared her throat. "Anton."

The historian stopped in mid-sentence and looked over his glass frames. "Yes? A question?"

"Not really a question." Lin folded her arms on the table. "It's the Stacey family I'm wondering about. I don't think they're related to the Coffins." When Lin spoke to Anton on the phone she'd told him that she was trying to recall information about the Stacey family because the name sounded familiar, but she couldn't place them and wondered if he could help.

Anton pushed his glasses to the bridge of his nose. "Right. I'm in the middle of writing a book about this side of the Coffin family and, well, you know how I am." He batted his hand in the air and then moved some papers to the side. He slid a different family tree forward. "Yes. Stacey. Another of the early founding families. One of them went on to found the Stacey chain of department stores." Anton followed a branch of a family line and then stopped. He looked at Lin. "Why are you asking about them?"

Lin told Anton about last night's cemetery visit. Anton knew that Lin could see ghosts so he wasn't alarmed when she described her late evening visit from the spirit she believed was Michael Sparrow. She also relayed her suspicions that the leg bone she'd found at the farmhouse might belong to the ghost.

Anton curled up his lip. He accepted ghostly visitations and Libby Hartnett's ability to sometimes "see" things, but grave robbing and discovering bones made him shudder. "Nasty business."

Lin told him about the cleverly adjusted gate on the Stacey mausoleum that slid back in order to give access to the door and the lock. "Which happened to be broken by the way."

"Did you go inside?" Little beads of perspiration showed on Anton's forehead.

Lin shook her head. "We left things as we found them and this morning Viv and I paid a visit to the police station. We told them what we found and that we suspected that the crypts inside the mausoleum may have been robbed. We left out who we suspect as robbers though."

"Probably wise." Anton dabbed his head with a napkin. "Not a good idea to accuse people without some evidence."

"So the Stacey family?" Lin encouraged the historian to continue.

Anton explained the different branches and what each line had accomplished on and off the island. Lin was about to interrupt again when Anton reached for a book and flipped the pages. "Here." He placed his finger on the page. "Yes, the Mid-Island Cemetery mausoleum has four members of the Stacey family entombed in it, a husband, wife, and two children who passed before reaching the age of eighteen. See here. The wife is Nora Stacey." Anton pointed to the diagram of the family trees. "She was a very distant relative of yours."

Lin's eyes widened in surprise.

"Nora Stacey was Emily Witchard Coffin's sister."

Lin's mouth dropped open. "Her sister? Then that's why Emily appears to me. That's why she wants me to help solve it." She raised her eyes to Anton and spoke softly. "I'd bet anything that someone stole Nora Stacey's bones. I'll bet all four family members' bones have been taken."

Anton dabbed his face again. "Oh, how disturbing." He had to sit down.

Lin turned the conversation to other topics so that Anton could focus on something pleasant.

Nicky got up from dozing when he sensed Anton's distress and went over and nudged at the man with his nose. Anton reached down and stroked the dog's smooth fur. Slowly, Anton relaxed.

Lin smiled at her smart little creature and gave him a wink.

***

Lin sat at a café table in the bookstore with Libby Hartnett and Viv and told them about the connection between Nora Stacey and Emily Coffin. She ran her finger over her horseshoe necklace and looked at Viv and Libby. "Which means Nora Stacey is a very distant relative of all of ours."

Viv opened her mouth to speak, but was so surprised by the news that she didn't know what to say.

"No wonder Emily wants you to help with this." Libby's blues eyes flashed. "Quinn is involved? I liked that young man." She shook her head. "I suppose greed can get the best of many."

"It was just too easy for him." Viv's lips were tight with disgust. "He had access and opportunity. We should have suspected him earlier."

"And this young woman, Chloe Waring. She seems involved from what you saw." Libby looked at Lin. "Quinn and his wife always seemed happy together. Why is he with this other woman?"

"Maybe they're just working together," Viv

suggested. "Maybe it's strictly business."

A cloud had settled over Libby's face. "What's the next step in getting some evidence that Quinn and Chloe Waring are the grave robbers?"

"I'm going out to Quinn's house tomorrow," Lin said. "He has a truck to sell and I'm in the market for one. It will give me a chance to see him interact with his wife and I can get a look around the place. Maybe something will stand out. Maybe I'll see something that can tie him to the crime."

"You're not going alone?" Libby was concerned for Lin's safety.

"Jeff is going with me. He can chat up Quinn while I glance around."

"Leave Nicky here with me tomorrow," Viv offered. "He hasn't visited with Queenie in a while. Then you can tell me what you found out when you come to pick him up."

"What about other suspects?" Libby asked.

"We suspected Jonas Bradley, too." Lin took a sip of her tea. "He's an odd one and he drove an older, dark sedan which looked a lot like the car Viv and I saw at the cemetery."

"But," Viv said, "he doesn't have the opportunity that Quinn has and the other day, we saw Chloe driving his dark-colored car. We wondered if she bought it from Jonas and is using it to transport bones from the cemetery."

Lin added, "Quinn seems the more likely suspect, but if he proves to be innocent then we'll take another look at Jonas."

John came around the corner, spotted the three women at the table, and sat down with them. He caught Mallory's eye and ordered a latte. The girls filled him in on what had been going on. They left out the parts about the ghosts.

"I know who Chloe Waring is." John's latte was delivered to the table. "She owns a boat down at the docks." John lived on his boat and knew or was familiar with many of the people who kept vessels. "She isn't on my dock, but I've seen her coming and going."

"Does she live on her boat?" Viv asked.

"I don't think so. Hers is like my boat so she could live on it, but I don't think she does. I think she lives in town. I'm not a hundred percent sure though."

Viv leaned in. "Whether she lives on it or not, having a boat is sure convenient, isn't it?"

Lin agreed. "She can use the boat to ferry the bones to the mainland. Keep them in suitcases. No one would ever know what she was up to."

John's phone buzzed and he read the incoming text. His eyebrows shot up and he looked at Viv and Lin. "You were right."

Viv cocked her head.

"It's my friend at the police station. Officers and a medical examiner went to the Mid-Island cemetery today. There'll be a press conference later. The Stacey mausoleum is empty."

The Haunted Bones

CHAPTER 24

Lin had arranged a meeting time with Quinn to take a look at the truck he had for sale. Jeff had to work on the other side of the island so he was going to meet Lin there. The road to Quinn's place went right by the farmhouse where Lin and Leonard had been working. The landscaping was almost complete and they were quite pleased with the way it had turned out.

Lin drove along thinking about the case and wondering if there would be anything at Quinn's house that might be used to tie him to the grave robberies. She knew it was a long shot since she couldn't just wander off by herself while she was there, but she hoped she might see or sense some small thing that could lead to evidence.

A half-mile from the farmhouse, the truck sputtered and wouldn't respond to Lin pushing on the gas pedal. Giving a few sporadic lurches, the engine let out a gasp and gave out. Lin braked and eased the old truck to the side of the road. Letting out a couple of curses, she turned the key in the ignition a few times only to be met with a grinding sound and then nothing. *Bah.*

Lin reached for her bag and took out her phone. She sent a text to Leonard asking if he was working at the farmhouse. She tapped her fingers on the steering wheel while waiting for a reply. When he didn't answer, she texted Jeff to let him know that the truck had died and that she was going to walk to the farmhouse to see if Leonard might still be working there. Lin would let Jeff know if she could get a ride from Leonard to meet him at Quinn's house. Setting down her phone on the passenger seat, she removed the keys from the ignition and put them in her bag.

Lin covered the half-mile quickly and walked down the farmhouse's long driveway. Leonard wasn't there. Sighing, she reached for her phone to text Quinn that she'd be late. Her hand fished around in her bag searching for the phone when Lin realized she'd left it in the truck. *What else can go wrong?*

She headed for the Sawyer's house next door to borrow their phone to call Jeff, and then she'd walk back to the truck to wait for him. Lin pushed through the brush and low-hanging branches to cut over to the Sawyer's house.

Clouds had rolled in blocking the sun and making the early evening darker than usual. A sense of unease pinged at Lin as she climbed the steps to the Sawyer's front door and pushed on the doorbell. Usually Olive opened the door within a few seconds which always made Lin feel like the woman had been spying on her, but today no one answered.

She pushed the bell again and waited. Nothing. Lin walked to the end of the porch and looked down the driveway. The two usual cars were parked in front of the garage.

Lin walked back to the door and knocked on it in case the bell didn't chime when she'd pushed it. The door opened a crack from the force of the knock. Lin's throat tightened. "Olive?" When there was no response from inside, Lin put her hand on the door and opened it a few inches. "Lloyd? Is anyone home? It's Lin Coffin." She peeked inside.

On the pale blue foyer floor tiles, were several large drops of blood. Lin sucked in a quick breath. "Olive?" She stood quietly at the door listening. The house was as quiet as a tomb.

Although Lin's first instinct was to run away as fast as she could, she worried that Olive and Lloyd were hurt inside so she took a hesitant first step into the entryway. She thought of finding the house phone and calling the police, but since she'd contacted the police twice already in the past days she thought she should look around first in case one of the Sawyers had only cut themselves and might be resting somewhere at the back of the house.

Lin wished Nicky was with her as she moved

quietly into the living room. Drops of blood on the wood floor led back out into the central hallway and Lin, with her heart pounding like a sledgehammer, followed them like breadcrumbs on a trail. She swallowed hard and moved down the hall looking in each room she passed on the way to the back of the house.

"Olive?" Lin's voice came out like a squeak. A trail of blood spots led to a room on the left off of the hallway. The door was closed. Lin knocked.

A creaking noise caused her to whirl around. The hall was empty and she let out a sigh. Old houses were always squeaking and groaning. Turning back to the door, she took hold of the knob and steeling herself to what she might find, pushed it open and stepped in. The room was beautifully decorated with expensive-looking cherry wood furniture and plush formal chairs. A massive desk stood in front of a huge window. Vases of flowers had been placed around the room.

Lin glanced about and then gasped. Lloyd was face-down on the floor to the left of the desk. Blood showed on the back of his head. She ran to the man, called his name, and gently shook his arm trying to rouse him. Putting her fingers on his neck, she felt a pulse and exhaled in relief, but then her heart sank. *Where was Olive?*

Lin stood, her eyes flashing about the room looking for the woman. On a plush high-backed chair that was facing towards the fireplace, she could see an elbow on the armrest. Waves of fear and anxiety washed over Lin and her head started to spin. She put her hand on the desk to steady herself. "Olive?" The word was barely audible.

Stepping closer to the chair, Lin could see lit candles of different sizes arranged inside the fireplace.

Her head spinning, she moved around the chair and what she saw caused her to stumble backwards so fast that she almost toppled over and crashed onto the fireplace hearth.

A skeleton sat in the chair wearing a long, worn, faded high-collared dress.

Lin had her hand over her mouth. She wasn't sure if she'd screamed or not. Staring at the body, her breath came in gasps and she blinked hard several times to be sure that what she thought she saw was really in the chair.

She careened like a drunken man to the desk and reached for the phone. Her hand froze. Out of the corner of her eye, Lin saw someone step into the room. "Olive."

Olive had a crazed gleam in her eye. "Don't touch that phone. Move away from the desk." The woman wore a black hoodie. She moved into the center of the room, holding the fireplace poker in her bloody hand. Lin thought Lloyd must have put up quite a fight.

"Lloyd's hurt. We need to call for help." Lin eyed Olive's other hand to see if she carried a gun or a knife. The hand was empty.

Olive cackled. "*I'm* the one who hurt him." Her face hardened as she looked at the man sprawled on the floor. "He couldn't let me do this. He had to interfere."

Lin wanted to get Olive talking, try to distract her. "What do you mean?"

Olive's wild eyes locked onto Lin. "You found my bone. You had to put your nose into my business. I wasn't hurting anything."

"You took the bodies from the mausoleums?" Lin tried to figure out how to get past Olive and out the door.

"It wasn't easy." Olive huffed. "But I did it."

"Why?" Lin shuffled a foot away from the desk.

"I honor the dead." Olive's chest was rapidly rising and falling. "It's my religion."

Lin gestured to the body in the chair. "Do you have others?"

"I'm leaving. I'm taking the precious ones with me. You can't stop me."

"I won't." Lin shook her head. "I won't stop you." She hoped Olive would take the skeleton and just go, but she knew in her heart that Olive wouldn't leave without trying to hurt her ... or worse. "I won't tell anyone."

Olive narrowed her eyes and took two steps forward. Lin's eyes darted around the space trying to figure out which side of the room she should run for.

"I know you'll tell," Olive sneered.

In a split second, Olive rushed forward. Lin grabbed a paperweight from the desktop. She hurled it at the charging woman, dashed around the back of the desk, jumped over Lloyd's body, and raced for the door.

Olive screeched like a banshee.

Lin bolted down the hallway to the front door, hurtled across the porch, and smacked right into Jeff just as Leonard crashed through the brush from the backyard of the farmhouse and ran across the lawn to them.

CHAPTER 25

Lin, Jeff, and Nicky walked under the white arbor covered with pink roses and up the steps to Viv's lovely gray-shingled Cape-style house. The door was open and Lin led the way inside carrying a veggie casserole. Leonard had arrived just before them and he stood with John admiring the antique map that Viv recently had framed and hung on the living room wall. The map was one of several found in Viv's storage room, hidden there hundreds of years ago by Sebastian Coffin. The maps were thought to have belonged to a famous pirate and supposedly showed where his loot was still hidden. The treasure was estimated to be worth a fortune in today's dollars.

Viv carried a drink to Leonard and took the platter he'd brought with him. "Someday Lin and I are going to go find that treasure and become billionaires."

"Yo ho ho. Try and stop us, matey." Lin sidled up to them to look over the map. "The map looks fabulous. The framing came out great."

She glanced at the tray in Viv's hands and then looked at Leonard. "You made these?"

Leonard gave a nod. "Mini spanakopita triangles."

Lin removed one from the plate and popped it into her mouth. Her eyes closed as she chewed. "These are amazing." She tilted her head, a wide grin on her face. "You never cease to surprise."

Leonard's cheeks tinged pink.

Everyone went out to the deck where appetizers were set up on a side table and drinks were arranged on a glass cart. The table was set with blue and white plates, blue napkins, and crystal glasses. Viv said, "We're celebrating the end of that awful case."

John was manning the grill and Jeff and Leonard stood on either side of him.

Viv rolled her eyes. "It must hark back to the days of early man. Light a fire outside and men must cook something."

Lin chuckled as she filled her small plate with appetizers. She watched Nicky and Queenie chase each other around the yard.

Viv spoke softly. "You should have seen those two when you were at the Sawyer's house. They acted crazy. Jumping at me, Nicky whining, Queenie hissing. I thought they'd contracted rabies." She shook her head. "Then I figured you must be in trouble so I called Leonard and said I was worried. I told him that you were supposed to call me and I hadn't heard from you. I'd been calling and calling you and you wouldn't answer. He called Jeff and the two converged on the Sawyer place."

Lin hugged her cousin. "Thank you."

"Thank those two nutty animals." Viv narrowed her eyes and whispered. "They must be psychic or something."

Jeff checked the meat on the grill. "Boy, that Sawyer woman was as crazy as an old bat. Imagine her breaking into tombs and removing bodies." He made a sound of disgust. "You wouldn't catch me within a mile of that sort of thing."

Libby Hartnett and Anton Wilson came down the driveway. Libby carried two homemade pies and Anton held a bag containing three kinds of ice cream and whipped cream.

Anton agreed with Jeff. "I am with you on that. Grave robbing. Ugh." His body gave a shudder.

Viv took the treats into the house to place them in the fridge and returned with cocktail glasses so that Jeff could make drinks for Libby and Anton.

"Just give me whiskey on the rocks." Anton sank into a deck chair. "I need a stiff drink after hearing what Olive Sawyer did."

A news conference had been held earlier in the day and the information had spread like wildfire all over the island. It seemed to be all anyone was talking about.

Libby repeated what she'd heard. "Mrs. Sawyer

wanted the bones as part of some religious thing she was into. She'd been reading up on ancient religious practices."

"She completely skewed what she read. She came up with the crazy idea of honoring the dead by keeping bones in her house." Anton shook his head and took a long swallow from his glass. "It is a misguided notion with no relation to anything except what she'd concocted in her head," Anton sputtered. His face was almost white.

"Olive was the one we saw at the cemetery that night." Viv turned to Lin. "She was driving an old car that Lloyd kept in their garage. She was wearing a hoodie. She saw us there so she pulled her car over on the fire road and came through the woods to see what we were up to. She saw us at the mausoleum. Then she drove on the fire road to the back of the cemetery office and went in to get the key to the crew's storage building where she got a new lock to put on the mausoleum. She changed the lock and put the new key in the office with the other crypt keys."

Lin added, "She also confessed to going into the cemetery office to access the files so she could figure out which mausoleums were old and probably contained the remains of people with no living relatives. That way there would be less chance that someone would notice the damaged locks." Lin sighed. "It wasn't hard for Olive to access the office since the key to the cottage was in the flower box at the back door."

Leonard asked, "Did Lloyd know what his wife was up to?"

"No," John answered. "Mr. Sawyer told police that his wife seemed to be becoming more and more obsessed with reading about different religions. She'd set up candles at what he described as make-shift shrines or little altars. He had no idea that she was out robbing graves. Mrs. Sawyer initially kept the bones in an old barn at the rear of their property. She also hid some in the farmhouse's backyard. Lloyd saw her over there one night and later went to inspect, but didn't find anything. He came home the other day to find a fully-clothed skeleton in his den. That's when Olive attacked him." John removed the grilled meat and vegetables and put them on a platter. "By the way, Olive's friend was a Realtor. That's how Olive knew that the house Lin found the partial skeleton in was empty."

Viv said, "And Olive tried to make you suspicious of Jonas Bradley to divert attention away from her."

"It worked, too," Lin groaned. "Then we got suspicious of Quinn. I feel really badly about that."

Jeff carried a platter of grilled chicken and beef to the deck. "It turns out that Quinn was buying Chloe's boat from her. It was a surprise gift for his wife."

Lin buried her face in her hands and muttered.

"I'm ashamed for suspecting them."

"Thank God is what I say." Libby sipped her drink. "I always liked Quinn. I was so disappointed that he might be involved in this grave robbery crime and was cheating on his wife. I'm going to maintain my trust in humanity by focusing on Quinn being a good person and chalking up the acts of Olive Sawyer to mental imbalance."

"Why was Quinn really making those trips to the mainland?" Leonard asked. "He'd told Lin he was taking care of business for some elderly people."

John chuckled. "He actually was. His father set up a foundation while he was alive to assist elderly people who had no family. Quinn was going to some meetings since he'd recently been named to the board of directors."

"I was wrong about everything," Lin said. "I'm never getting involved in a case again."

Viv made eye contact with her cousin knowing full well that if a ghost required help, then Lin would do whatever she could to assist.

"The case is solved because of you." Leonard raised a glass and Lin reluctantly clinked with him. "Maybe you didn't figure it out, but because of your involvement those bones and skeletons are back where they belong."

"Here, here." Anton raised his glass. "To Carolin, Nantucket's honorary snoop ... I mean detective." He grinned.

Jeff put his arm around Lin and gave her a sweet

kiss. "The only thing that matters is that she's safe and sound."

Everyone gathered around the table and dug into the delicious food. Conversation flowed from one topic to another and laughter filled the night air. Nicky and Queenie ate cut up pieces of grilled chicken from blue plates that Lin had set in the grass by the deck. After putting down the plates, she gave each of them a cheek scratch and whispered, "Thanks for watching out for me." Lin could have sworn that the gray cat gave her a wink.

When the meal was over, they all pitched in carrying leftovers and dirty dishes into the house. Dishes were rinsed and placed in the dishwasher. Libby took the ice cream from the freezer and removed the pies and whipped cream from the fridge. Anton put coffee on and set a kettle on the burner for tea.

Lin carried a tray of dessert dishes and napkins outside to the deck. As she was setting the table, a freezing whoosh of cold air swept over her. She turned slowly and looked across the yard. Six ghosts stood shimmering in the moonlight with Emily Coffin in the middle of them. They all made eye contact with Lin and one by one, nodded their heads to her. Lin's eyes filled with tears and she blinked them back so she could watch the ghostly atoms swirling faster and faster until they all disappeared.

Lin brushed at her eyes. Turning to go back

inside, she caught sight of Leonard standing at the corner of the house holding Queenie. Nicky sat at the man's feet. The three of them were staring at the spot in the backyard where the spirits had just appeared.

"Leonard?" Lin said.

"Oh, Coffin." He carried the cat up to the deck and set her down. Nicky ran up the steps and sat next to Queenie. "When I brought the mugs and tea cups out, I wondered where the animals had got to. Viv said she wanted them to stay in the yard, so I went around the house to the side yard to look for them." Leonard smiled at Lin. "And here they are."

Lin stared at the man wondering why he and the dog and the cat were looking into the rear yard at the very moment the spirits made their appearance. She cocked her head suspiciously at Leonard and was about to question him when he spoke.

"It's chilly now," Leonard said. "I think I'll get my jacket from the house." As he was passing Lin, he gave her a smile and his eyes twinkled. "Come on, Coffin. You better get your sweater. You never know when a cold breeze might come through." Leonard went inside leaving the young woman staring after him.

Through the open windows, Lin could hear everyone chatting happily in the kitchen as they cleaned up and got the dessert, coffee and tea ready. The sound of them made her heart swell.

Before going in to join the others, Lin took one

more look to where the ghosts had stood in the yard, and she smiled.

THANK YOU FOR READING!

BOOKS BY J.A. WHITING CAN BE FOUND HERE:

www.amazon.com/author/jawhiting

To hear about new books and book sales, please sign up for my mailing list at:

www.jawhitingbooks.com

Your email will never be sold, shared, or spammed.

BOOKS BY J. A. WHITING

LIN COFFIN COZY MYSTERIES

A Haunted Murder (A Lin Coffin Cozy Mystery Book 1)
A Haunted Disappearance (A Lin Coffin Cozy Mystery Book 2)
The Haunted Bones (A Lin Coffin Cozy Mystery Book 3)
And more to come!

SWEET COVE COZY MYSTERIES

The Sweet Dreams Bake Shop (Sweet Cove Cozy Mystery Book 1)
Murder So Sweet (Sweet Cove Cozy Mystery Book 2)
Sweet Secrets (Sweet Cove Cozy Mystery Book 3)
Sweet Deceit (Sweet Cove Cozy Mystery Book 4)
Sweetness and Light (Sweet Cove Cozy Mystery Book 5)
Home Sweet Home (Sweet Cove Cozy Mystery Book 6)
Sweet Fire and Stone (Sweet Cove Cozy Mystery Book 7)
And more to come!

OLIVIA MILLER MYSTERIES

J.A Whiting

The Killings (Olivia Miller Mystery Book 1)
Red Julie (Olivia Miller Mystery Book 2)
The Stone of Sadness (Olivia Miller Mystery Book 3)

If you enjoyed the book, please consider leaving a review.

A few words are all that's needed.

It would be very much appreciated.

J.A Whiting

ABOUT THE AUTHOR

J.A. Whiting lives with her family in New England. Whiting loves reading and writing mystery stories.

VISIT ME AT:

www.jawhitingbooks.com

www.facebook.com/jawhitingauthor

www.amazon.com/author/jawhiting

Printed in Great Britain
by Amazon